SBN 361 01384 1

This edition copyright © 1969 Walt Disney Productions. Published by Purnell & Sons Ltd., London, W1A 2LG.
Printed by Purnell & Sons Ltd., Paulton, Somerset.
Reprinted 1970, 1971 (twice)

Walt Disney's GIANT STORY BOOK

PURNELL

London

CONTENTS

WALT DISNEY'S
MARY POPPINS

AN EAST wind was blowing over Cherry Tree Lane, where Jane and Michael Banks lived with their parents, Mr. and Mrs. Banks. Besides there was Katie Nanna, the nursemaid, who doesn't really count because at the time the east wind blew she was leaving Number Seventeen.

The wind was whipping gustily through the leaves as Katie Nanna came stamping down the stairs with her bags, hopped into the waiting hansom cab and rode away, leaving Jane and Michael Banks without a nanny.

Mr. Banks was a very busy man. He never had time for any fun, but he *did* know his duty to wife and family. He wrote an advertisement to the *Times*. And the next morning a line of applicants stretched down the Banks' front walk all the way to the Lane.

Jane and Michael looked down from the nursery window. "They're horrible!" said Michael with a shudder. But as the children watched, the east wind started up again,

blowing through the branches of the cherry trees in the Lane. And it tweaked at their hats and snatched at their umbrellas and blew all those would-be nannies away! Yes, over the fence posts, over the tree tops, quite out of sight they flew!

Then down over the park, swinging gently back and forth as she held to the handle of her umbrella, a marvelous person came floating on the wind. "It's she!" gasped Jane at the nursery window. "She's just the one we wanted." And as they watched, the person floated down to the front porch, put down her carpet bag, closed her umbrella, and rang the front door bell. That was how Mary Poppins came to Jane and Michael Banks on the east wind.

While Jane and Michael watched in astonishment from the nursery landing, Mary Poppins slid gracefully up the banister and set down her carpet bag. The children could see that it was empty. But from the empty carpet bag she took one hat rack, one large, gilt-edged mirror, a rubber plant and a lighted floor lamp!

"There!" she said, looking around the room. "That's a bit more comfortable, I would say!"

"Now," said Mary Poppins with a look around the nursery, "it's time for a game called Tidy up the Nursery."

"I don't like the sound of it," said Michael. But Mary Poppins only smiled.

"In every job that must be done," she said, "we find an element of fun. We find the fun and *snap!* the job's a game!"

And when Mary Poppins snapped her fingers, all Jane's dolls settled themselves neatly on the nursery shelves. Michael's soldiers, made of lead, marched to tents beneath the bed. Toys and clowns and wood blocks flew into their magic box. Shirts and skirts and waistcoats, too, soared to closets out of view. In no time at all, the nursery was tidy. "That's better," Mary Poppins sniffed. "Now it looks less like a bear pit."

"Let's do it again," said Michael.

"Nonsense," said Mary Poppins. "It is time for an outing in the park. Come along," she said. "Spit-spot!"

In the park they met Bert, the jack-of-all-trades. He was down on his knees drawing pictures in colored chalks on the sidewalk. Jane and Michael stooped down to look at each picture.

"Oh here's a lovely one," sighed Jane. "I wish we could go there."

"A typical English countryside," Bert pointed out with pardonable pride. "Quite a suitable spot for travel and high adventure. Why not? And down the road there's a country fair. Come along." And taking each child by a hand he winked at them. "Bit of magic," he explained. "It's easy. You wink. . . . You think. . . . You do a double blink. . . . You close your eyes and—jump!"

With a sniff Mary Poppins put up her umbrella, and away they all floated straight into the drawing of the English countryside.

It was a beautiful spot, green and quiet and sparkling with sun.

"Mary Poppins," said Bert, "you look beautiful!" And so she did, for suddenly she was dressed in the height of fashion, from the wide curly brim of her hat to the diamond buttons on her shoes.

"You look fine too, Bert," said Mary Poppins. And so he did, in a new suit of clothes and a new straw hat.

"I thought you said there was a fair," said Michael, who was not impressed by clothes, though he looked very fine himself.

"So I did," said Bert. "Just down the road and over the hill."

Bert gave Mary Poppins his arm, and off they all strolled through the countryside. All the birds and animals came out to greet Mary—the lambs and the cows and the old gray horse, the geese and the turtles in the pond. The whole world seemed to dance for joy, and along with Bert the animals sang, "Any day with Mary is a jolly holiday."

In a sunny spot among the trees they found a tea pavilion, where they stopped for a lovely afternoon tea. The waiters looked exactly like penguins.

When their tea was finished, they waltzed away, down the road and over the hill to the merry-go-round. It slowed down just as they approached it, and they leaped aboard. Each

one landed gracefully in the saddle of a wooden horse.

"Imagine!" said Jane. "Our own private merry-go-round."

"It's very nice," said Bert, putting on airs, "very nice indeed, if you don't want to go anywhere."

"Who says we are not going anywhere?" said Mary Poppins with a toss of her head. And she had a quiet word with the guard.

"Right-o, Mary Poppins," smiled the guard, and he lifted his cap. Then he pulled the tallest lever on the merry-go-round machine—and away went their horses *tum-tum-tee-tum* across the countryside.

From the distance came the sound of a hunting horn. "Follow me!" called Mary Poppins over her shoulder. And away they rode to the sound of the horn, passing the huntsmen one and all. They even started to pass the fox, until Bert scooped him up and gave him a ride.

Jane and Michael were riding so hard and fast that at first they did not notice that Mary Poppins had left their side. Then, "It's a race!" cried Michael. "And look, Bert!" cried Jane. "Mary Poppins is winning!" "So she is!" said Bert.

There came the leaders, pounding down the track. And as Jane and Michael watched, the riders pulled aside, letting Mary Poppins ride between them straight to the finish line.

Jane and Michael were sitting on the fence with Bert, eating taffy apples, when the first big round raindrops fell. Then came a flash of lightning, and the rain came pouring down!

"Michael! Jane! Don't run about. Stay close to me," called Mary Poppins. As they huddled close together under her umbrella, all the countryside around them seemed to melt away. . . . They were back in the park! And on the pavement at their feet Bert's drawings were melting into bright puddles of rain.

"Spit-spot," said Mary Poppins. "Hurry along, children, or we'll be late for tea. Good-bye, Bert." And soon they were snug

in the nursery with a fire glowing in the fireplace.

On the hearth stood Jane's and Michael's shoes, drying out from their day in the rain. Beside them leaned Mary Poppins' umbrella. Tea was over and Mary Poppins was tucking Jane and Michael into bed.

"Mary Poppins, you won't ever leave us, will you?" Jane said sleepily. "Will you stay," begged Michael, "if we promise to be good?" "That's a pie-crust promise," said Mary Poppins. "Easily made, easily broken. I shall stay until the wind changes." And that was all that she would say.

The next thing Jane and Michael knew, Mary Poppins was opening the curtains. "Up, up!" she ordered. "No dawdling. It's a glorious day—super-cali-fragil-istic, I might

say. We're going for a walk. Spit-spot. This way."

"Super-cali-fragil-istic," sang Jane and Michael as they danced along the walk. They almost bumped into Mary Poppins when she stopped to speak to a little dog. The children had never seen the dog before, but Mary Poppins seemed to know him well. She called him Andrew. The little dog barked noisily at Mary Poppins. "Again?" said Mary Poppins. "I'll go straight away."

Taking Jane and Michael by the hand, Mary Poppins started off the way Andrew had come. And in no more than a moment or two she was rapping at the door of a small, quaint house.

It was Bert who opened the door. "How is he?" Mary Poppins asked. "Never seen him

like this," said Bert soberly, "and that's the truth." He pushed the door wide open. Jane and Michael peeked in.

A large, cheerful room lay before them. In the center stood a table laid for tea. "Bless— bless my soul," said a voice rich with chuckles. "Is that Mary Poppins? I'm delighted to see you."

The voice came from above. They looked up, and there in the air sat Mary Poppins' Uncle Albert, chuckling merrily.

"You have just got to stop laughing, Uncle Albert," said Mary Poppins sternly. "I know my dear, but I do enjoy it so," said Uncle Albert. Here the chuckles bubbled out so that he bobbed against the ceiling. "And the moment I start laughing—hee hee—it's all *up* with me."

He looked so comic that Jane and Michael, though they were trying hard to be polite, just couldn't help doing what they did. They began to chuckle.

By now Bert was rolling about, shaking with laughter. Soon he rose from the floor and was bobbing about beside Uncle Albert. At the sight of him, Jane and Michael found themselves simply filled with laughter, too. They grew lighter and lighter until their heads bumped the ceiling! Only Mary Poppins remained firmly on the ground.

"You're the silliest things I've ever seen," said Mary Poppins severely from below, "or my name isn't Mary Poppins."

"Speaking of names," said Bert, "I know a man with a wooden leg named Smith . . ."

"Really?" chuckled Uncle Albert. "What's

the name of his other leg?" And they all roared with laughter, bouncing in the air.

"Now then, Jane, Michael! It's time for tea," said Mary Poppins.

"Won't you pour out, Mary Poppins?" asked Uncle Albert.

At that the tea table came soaring through the air and Mary Poppins rose sedately to sit near the tea pot.

"I'm having such a good time, my dear," said Uncle Albert as they laughed their way through tea. "I wish you could all stay up here with me always."

"We'll jolly well have to," grinned Michael. "There's no way to get down."

"Well, to be honest," said Uncle Albert, "there *is* a way. Think of something sad and down you go."

"Time to go home." Mary Poppins' voice sounded like a trumpet above all the laughter in the room.

And at that saddest thought of all, down they all came with a bump.

Back home, Jane and Michael tried to tell Mr. Banks about the wonderful tea party and the laughing and the man with the wooden leg named Smith. But he did not seem to understand.

"Poppins," he said severely, "I'm disappointed in you. I am disturbed to hear my children speak about popping in and out of chalk pavement-drawings. Fox hunts, race tracks, tea parties on the ceiling—highly questionable outings. Words like super-cali-fra-craj-uh—"

"Super-cali-fragil-istic," said Mary Poppins.

"Of course. Thank you," said Mr. Banks. "Now if they must go on outings, they should have a purpose. They must learn of solid things, like banking. . . ."

"I understand," said Mary Poppins. "Tomorrow, freshly pressed and neatly dressed, Jane and Michael will be at your side."

"At my side?" cried Mr. Banks. "Where are we going?"

"To the bank, of course," said Mary Poppins. "Just as you proposed."

Jane and Michael could scarcely believe their ears. An outing with their father!

"Yes," said Mary Poppins, "and on the way to the bank you'll see the old bird lady on the steps of St. Paul's selling her bags of crumbs. 'Feed the birds, feed the birds, tuppence the bag,' she cries. And all around the cathedral, the Saints and Apostles look down, and they smile when someone shows he cares—with tuppence for a bag of crumbs."

Next morning, just as Mary Poppins had promised, Jane and Michael did see the old bird lady on the cathedral steps. "Feed the birds! Tuppence the bag," she cried.

"Please, father, may we feed the birds?" asked Jane.

"I've got tuppence from my money box," said Michael. "It's just as Mary Poppins says."

"I am not interested in what Mary Poppins says," said Mr. Banks. "When we get to

the bank, I shall show you what may be done with tuppence."

The bank was a great and awesome place. No one spoke above a whisper, so it seemed. Soon Michael and Jane were being presented to the Senior Mr. Dawes. He was a very, very old gentleman, gray and wrinkled and pinched and musty. He was the head of the bank.

"These are my children, Mr. Dawes," said Mr. Banks. "They wish to open an account."

"Oh, capital, capital!" said Mr. Dawes. "How much money have you, young man?"

"Tuppence," said Michael. "But I want it to feed the birds."

"Fiddlesticks," said Mr. Dawes. "Feed the birds and what have you got? Fat birds! But put your money in the bank, and safe and sound as the turn of a crank, your tuppence will draw interest and compound. You'll

have railways, you'll have ships, river dams and ocean trips . . ." And he snatched Michael's tuppence from his hand.

"No!" said Michael. "I want to feed the birds. Give me back my tuppence!" And he snatched his tuppence back and ran.

"Michael! Jane!" shouted Mr. Banks angrily. But it was too late. The children had dashed out of the bank.

Jane and Michael ran up streets, down alleys, through the strange and busy ways of London Town.

As the children rounded a corner, not knowing where they were, a strange figure appeared before them, smudged with soot and bristling with brooms. It reached out both arms to them.

"Let us go!" cried Michael. "Let my sister alone."

"Easy now! Your old friend Bert isn't going to harm you."

DISNEY G.S. BK—B

And Bert it was, dressed as a chimney sweep. "Now," he asked, "who's after you?"

"Father is," said Jane. "He's furious."

"Now, now," said Bert. "There must be some mistake. Your father is a fine gentleman who loves you. He's the one you should feel sorry for, working in that cold, heartless bank all day."

"Oh, Bert," said Jane. "Do you think father needs our help?"

"I'll give him my tuppence," said Michael with a sigh.

It was late afternoon when Bert came home with Michael and Jane, into Cherry Tree Lane. They had had a fine frolic on the way with a whole band of chimney sweeps. Over the rooftops they had gone, and the sweeps were just dancing on their way when Mr. Banks came home.

"What's all this?" cried Mr. Banks as the sweeps danced past him.

"Oh, Father," said Jane. "I'm so glad you got home in time. Every one of those chimney sweeps shook your hand, so you're going to be very lucky."

"That may well be," said Mr. Banks. "I explained to the men at the bank, you see, about Mary Poppins and the bird woman, and Uncle Albert and the laughing, and the man with the wooden leg named Smith . . . and the whole super-cali-fragil-istic thing. And they all laughed. Even old Mr. Dawes laughed—it's the first time I've ever seen such a thing!"

Just then a brisk wind whipped around the corner. At Number Seventeen, Cherry Tree Lane, Mary Poppins stood at the window and sniffed at the breeze. In the street below she could see Mr. Banks, an arm around each child.

"I see the wind has changed," said Mary Poppins to herself. "It's time to go."

And as Mr. Banks and the children came up the front steps, Mary Poppins, properly dressed in her hat and coat, and carpet bag in hand, opened her umbrella. The wind slipped under it and away she flew—over the front gate, over the branches of the cherry trees in the lane.

"She's going, Jane," said Michael tearfully.

"Don't cry, children," said Mr. Banks. "She may be back. Let's give her a splendid send-off. Let's fly our kites!"

"You'll fly kites with us?" said Michael.

"By all means," said Mr. Banks happily.

And soon he and the children—and even Mrs. Banks—had kites flying high in the windy sky to wave Mary Poppins on her way.

DUMBO OF THE CIRCUS

THE CIRCUS ANIMALS paced back and forth in their cages nervously. They sniffed the air for the first smells of spring and peered at the skies anxiously.

Everyone in the circus was eager for spring to come. After long months at winter quarters in Florida, the clowns, the ringmaster, the musicians, the acrobats and the animal trainers were restless.

The trapeze artists were limbering up their muscles for their daredevil tricks. The circus train's locomotive, Casey Jr., was exercising his piston rods, and the calliope was practicing a few toots on his pipes. Before long, Casey Jr. would take the circus on tour.

They all stopped occasionally to look at the sky. They were expecting something!

Finally it came—a great flock of storks carrying big bundles in their beaks. The messenger birds zoomed low over the circus and dropped their packages. Parachutes blossomed forth, and the eagerly awaited bundles floated gently to earth.

When each bundle had been delivered safely, the circus animals were happy!

Leo Lion and his wife had four of the cutest cubs anyone had ever seen—

Mrs. Chimpanzee had a baby chimpanzee to dandle on her knees—

There was a tiny hippopotamus weighing only three hundred pounds—

An infant seal had come, as long as your hand and as bright as a cricket—

There was a baby tiger who loved to have his mother, Mrs. Tiger, polish his fur with her clean, soft tongue—

And two miniature zebras had come, complete with stripes—

But for Mrs. Jumbo, the elephant, who had been waiting so patiently, there was *nothing!* She scanned the sky for one of the messenger birds. As she waited, Mrs. Jumbo stamped nervously in her stall. Her elephant friends tried to comfort her, as much as possible. But it was difficult, for they were almost as disappointed as she was.

"Maybe the messenger's just a little late," one of the elephants said to Mrs. Jumbo. "Even a baby elephant is a heavy bundle for a stork, you know."

Mrs. Jumbo did not give up hope until the circus train pulled up on the loading platform and the animals marched into their cars. It was a happy time for everyone but the elephants. They did not want to go on tour without a baby elephant!

Casey Jr., the circus train locomotive, was not worrying about baby elephants. He blinked his lamps, stretched his piston rods to get the cramps out of them, blew the rust out of his whistle and a few experimental smoke rings out of his stack, and looked back to see how far the loading of the circus train had progressed. He whistled impatiently and shot a hiss of steam from his boiler to let everyone know he was ready.

"All aboard!" called the circus boss.

"All aboard!" whistled Casey, as he crouched low, pushed his wheels against the tracks, and pulled forward. The cars jerked into movement behind him, and he puffed away from the winter quarters, gaining speed and rolling along more and more easily.

Casey Jr. let out a long, high whistle. It was good to feel the cool fresh air rushing past him as he sped northward. He tooted a

21

greeting to some birds who flew alongside him. He whistled to the cows in a field, who looked up and mooed to him, as they did every spring, when Casey Jr. passed.

As he rattled across the plains, the young colts in the pastures challenged him to races. Casey Jr. purposely slowed down to let them beat him in order not to hurt their feelings. This pleased the colts' mothers, who looked on proudly and decided that Casey Jr. was a grand fellow.

On and on the little locomotive chugged, tooting at steamboats when he ran alongside rivers, and at factories when he passed through cities. They whistled back, for they were all old friends of Casey Jr. Casey had serious responsibilities, too. In the mountains, when he saw a tunnel ahead, he had to toot a warning to the giraffes to pull their necks down. And there was one particularly long, dark tunnel where he wasn't exactly afraid, but it somehow kept up his courage to whistle to himself a little.

In the train behind him, clowns sang in time to the clickety-clack of the wheels, and the animals rocked their babies to sleep with the swaying motion of their cars. But in the elephant car, Mrs. Jumbo stayed alone in her compartment, and her friends stood together without chattering and gossiping as they usually did.

Mrs. Jumbo would have been much happier if she had known who was sitting on a cloud not far away.

It was a special delivery stork! He had detoured around a bad thunderstorm and had lost his way. But here he was at last, on the trail of Mrs. Jumbo. Far below, he could see the circus train crawling across the country.

"Look out below!" he cried, as he picked up his bundle and descended in a power dive.

"Mrs. Jumbo? Where's Mrs. Jumbo?" he called as he came up to the two giraffes, who pointed to the elephant car ahead.

"Oh, Mrs. Jumbo!" sang the stork.

"In here!" cried the elephants. "In here! This way, please!"

The stork flew through the opening in the roof into the car where Mrs. Jumbo was so eagerly waiting for him.

"Mrs. Jumbo?" the stork said, tipping his cap politely, and putting his bundle on the floor beside her.

Mrs. Jumbo started at once to untie it, but the messenger insisted that Mrs. Jumbo sign the receipt for one elephant before she opened the package. Then he tipped his hat and flew away, as all the other elephants gathered round excitedly.

"Quick, open the bundle, Mrs. Jumbo!" cried one of the elephants.

"I'm on pins and needles!" cooed another.

"This is a proud, proud day for us elephants," said a third.

And when Mrs. Jumbo's trembling trunk had at last unfastened the bundle, there lay a little elephant all curled up asleep.

"Isn't he a darling?" cooed one of the elephants to the others.

"Just too sweet for words," said another.

Mrs. Jumbo just beamed at the little fellow.

"What are you going to name him?" asked the first elephant.

"Little Jumbo," said the mother proudly.

"Kootchie, kootchie, kootchie!" went one elephant, as she tickled the baby playfully.

That made him sneeze! And when the baby sneezed, his ears, which had been hidden, flapped forward.

The elephants jumped back in amazement! Those were the most enormous ears anyone had ever seen on an elephant. They were larger by far than the ears on all the grown-up elephants! They could not help staring at the baby elephant. Even Mrs. Jumbo looked startled and amazed.

The baby elephant looked up and smiled. His ears dropped back down again and

dragged on the floor. One of the big elephants tittered.

"Isn't he silly looking?" she whispered to the elephant next to her, but in a whisper so loud that everyone heard.

"Simply ridiculous!" said the other. "Why, he's just a freak elephant, that's all."

Mrs. Jumbo glared at them, and beamed at her baby. When he grew into those ears he would be the biggest and most magnificent elephant in the world.

"I think you'd better change his name," said the oldest elephant, trying to make her voice sound especially sweet. "Jumbo won't quite fit, I think *Dumbo* is what you mean."

All the other elephants giggled and laughed merrily over this clever joke. But Mrs. Jumbo could stand it no longer. She slammed her compartment door in their faces.

Through the walls, the mother elephant heard the others laughing and joking. She lay down and took her little baby in her arms, caressing him gently with her trunk. The baby elephant made small contented noises and gradually fell asleep.

Everyone in the circus called the baby elephant Dumbo. His big ears became the great joke of the circus. Every time the train went through a tunnel, a clown said he hoped Dumbo had pulled his ears in first. When the wind blew strongly, the big elephants tried to act worried, saying that if the wind caught Dumbo's ears, it would pick up the whole train and blow it away.

Dumbo just smiled when he heard these things. He was just a little bewildered that others were not more friendly with him. He even laughed at some of the jokes himself. He thought that the idea of flying away in the wind was fine—it sounded like fun.

Mrs. Jumbo stayed in her own compartment almost all the time, and kept little Dumbo with her. Her temper grew worse, and she began to brood and worry. And it is not good for elephants to brood and worry.

An evening finally came when everyone forgot about Dumbo. That was when Casey Jr. puffed wearily to a stop in the city where the first show was to be given. It had been a long pull for Casey Jr., but despite his fatigue he was excited, too. Even the storm that was raging could not dampen the spirits of the members of the circus. They set to work in the driving rain to raise the tents and get everything ready for the first show, which was to be given the next day.

The roustabouts opened the doors of the freight cars and began to unload the tents and the ropes. The animal keepers led out the elephants and set them to work. The big animals lifted the tent poles in their trunks and carried them to the middle of the open lot. They pushed the circus wagons off the flat cars and pulled the heavy loads that men could not possibly handle. And all the time

they worked, the rain poured down on them and the thunder boomed.

When the lightning flashed, Dumbo could see short glimpses of the hurried work going on all around him. When the thunder rumbled he just grasped his mother's tail a little more firmly and kept on trudging behind her. Wherever she went, lifting, pulling, and hauling, he tagged along.

As the sun rose in the morning, the clouds were chased from the sky by a fresh wind, and the circus, all set and ready for the first show, glistened in the bright morning light.

After breakfast, everyone got ready for the big parade. The clowns put on their wigs and make-up and costumes. The horses were brushed until they shone, and bright ribbons were put on their manes and tails. The animals marched into their cage-wagons, and the elephants got in line, tail and trunk, tail and trunk. The calliope brought up the rear, his shining pipes uttering little toots of impatience. This first parade of the season was his first chance to play those tunes that delighted the children lining the streets.

Finally the parade began. Bright flags were flying and hundreds of cheering people lined the streets. Boys and girls, men and women, grandmothers and grandfathers and babies in their mother's arms, were all there, cheering as the beautiful white horses appeared at the head of the parade. Everyone cried with pleasure as the well-trained animals pranced and reared back gracefully.

Next came the first group of clowns, jumping and leaping and running in circles. Then the big cage-wagons with the wild animals rolled into view, followed by more clowns. In the distance people could hear the shrieking song of the calliope, and they knew that the end of the circus was approaching. But first came the elephants, marching majestically down the center of the street. They kept perfect step as they walked along, each elephant holding with his trunk the tail of the elephant in front of him. At the very end of the line came Dumbo. He had a hard time reaching up with his trunk to the tail of his mother in front of him. And he could not keep step, no matter how hard he tried.

At first glance people thought Dumbo was cute. But when they saw his floppy ears dragging on the ground, they tittered and giggled and some laughed out loud. The people laughed at Dumbo more than they had at the monkeys or the clowns. Monkeys and clowns are supposed to be laughed at, but elephants are dignified and majestic creatures. You can say "Oh!" or "Ah!" or "How big!" or "How strong!" about an elephant, but you just can't laugh at him.

Poor Mrs. Jumbo's ears burned to hear all the laughter over her little son. She glared furiously at the people on the sidewalks. She was glad when the parade was ended. But she did not know that even worse was in store for her and for Dumbo.

Back in the tent, Mrs. Jumbo gave Dumbo a bath so that he would look fine for the first show that afternoon. She scrubbed him with her trunk until he laughed and said it tickled. He splashed in his tub and made his own shower bath by taking water in his trunk and spouting it into the air over him.

When Mrs. Jumbo had carefully wrung out Dumbo's big ears and he had shaken himself dry, they ate their lunch and then went to their stalls in the menagerie. The other animals had taken their places, the performers were all ready, and the ringmaster had shined up his black top hat. Outside the big tent, the barkers were shouting to the first of the crowd, telling of the wonderful sights to be seen inside—the fat lady, the thin man, Stretcho the india-rubber man, the man who swallowed sharp swords, the man who ate fire, the lions, the tigers, the acrobats, the clowns, and the elephants.

Soon the crowd was streaming through the tents. A group of boys gathered near the rope in front of Mrs. Jumbo's stall. They pointed at Dumbo and laughed. Dumbo, trying to be friendly, walked toward them, but at the very first step he tripped on one ear and rolled on the ground. The little boys roared with laughter.

"What a wonderful sailboat he'd make," yelled one boy.

Another boy opened his coat and held it far out from his body.

"Look! Here's Dumbo!" he cried, as he wiggled his coat and everyone laughed.

Mrs. Jumbo could stand no more. She reached out quickly and grabbed one boy—who had just been sticking out his tongue at Dumbo. Then she spanked him soundly! The other boys screamed and ran away, and the keepers came running as fast as they could.

"Wild elephant!" someone yelled, and the crowd began to run for the exits.

When the first of the animals' keepers tried to push Mrs. Jumbo back into the corner of her stall, she picked him up with her trunk and tossed him into a pile of hay. The ringmaster came with a whip, and Mrs. Jumbo threw him into a big tub of water.

More keepers came running with their long, spiked poles. They poked Mrs. Jumbo, trying to force her back in her stall, where they could tie her fast. But now the mother elephant knew that they wanted to lock her up, away from her little Dumbo. She lifted her trunk and bellowed loudly. She knocked down the keepers in front of her.

But a man slipped behind her and quickly put a chain around her rear leg. Then other men rushed forward and bound her.

"Take her to the prison car!" cried the dripping ringmaster. "She's dangerous!"

So Mrs. Jumbo was led away to prison and Dumbo was left all alone. He didn't have anybody at all.

That night in the elephant tent, all the big animals were gathered around a pile of hay for dinner. They were busy eating and talking about the terrible things that had happened that day.

"I used to think he was funny," one of them said. "But now I think he's a disgrace. Mrs. Jumbo was a fine, decent, and respectable elephant until he came along."

"Dumbo is not just a disgrace to his mother," said another. "He's a disgrace to all elephants the world over."

On the other side of the pile of hay was a very tiny creature who listened wonderingly to their conversation. It was Timothy, the circus mouse. He had smoothed out a comfortable bed for himself, and was lying there wondering how soon he should step out and scare the elephants. As long as he lived, he never stopped getting a thrill out of scaring elephants. Whoever it was that arranged

things so that elephants were frightened of mice had a great idea.

When Timothy was feeling a little blue, whenever he had a bad day—he could always make himself feel fine and important again just by scaring a bunch of elephants.

But today Timothy cocked his head on one side and listened carefully to the chatter of the big animals. Ordinarily the elephants didn't talk much while they were eating. Now they muttered and whispered in shocked tones, and Timothy guessed that they were really enjoying the whole affair even though they pretended to be horrified.

Something exciting had happened, anyway, Timothy concluded. Too bad he had missed it, whatever it was. It must have occurred while he was away searching for furniture for the new house he was building under the floor of the ringmaster's car. He stuck his head out of the hay to hear what the elephants were saying.

Then Dumbo came in, looking for something to eat. He smiled cheerfully up at the big elephants, for he was very lonesome. But when they saw him, they stopped talking at once, turned their backs on him, and closed the space around the pile of hay. The smile faded from Dumbo's face, tears came to his eyes, and he turned slowly away.

Now Timothy Mouse knew what the elephants were talking about. And when he saw Dumbo's ears he knew why.

"They can't do that to a little fellow," he muttered, "no matter who he is."

He brushed off his little red jacket, set his red bandmaster's cap at a jaunty angle, and leaped among the elephants.

"Boo!" he yelled, as loudly as he could.

The elephants jumped back, and looked at the tiny mouse with terror in their eyes. The tent became a mass of rushing elephants, bellowing, running, stamping, and squealing. One elephant ran up a ladder, and two of them even scurried up the tent poles. When

they were all just as far from the mouse as they could get, Timothy stood in the middle of the floor, put his hands on his hips, and glared around at them all.

"Pick on a little fellow, will you?" he cried. "You ought to be ashamed of yourselves! With all those big bodies you've got, you'd think there'd be a little heart in them. But no, not you! Just appetite and gossip, that's all. You wouldn't even let the little guy have something to eat. You made fun of him and called him names. You probably did the same thing to his mother and drove her wild. And why? Just because he was born a little different from you, that's all. Sure, I can figure it out. He's got big ears. So what of it? I'll bet he's got a heart inside of him, and that counts. It's more than you've got."

He paused for breath and looked around.

"Boo!" Timothy Mouse yelled again. "Boo! Boo! Get out of here!"

With a yell of fright, the terrified elephants dashed out of the tent.

Timothy knew it would be at least a half hour before they were all rounded up and brought back again. He smiled to himself and looked around for Dumbo.

"Hey, little fellow, where are you? Where are you, Dumbo?" he called.

Then he saw the tip of a little trunk waving from under a bale of hay. Timothy walked over and patted the trunk.

"No need to be afraid, Dumbo," he said. "Come on out. That's just an act I put on for those big fellows."

Dumbo had been afraid. But when he had listened to Timothy Mouse telling those great big elephants how mean they were, when he had heard the mouse telling them all it didn't make any difference just because he had big ears, Dumbo's heart had been warmed as never before.

"It's lucky for you I came along," said Timothy, "because I'm the one to help you out of your troubles. You leave all your troubles to Timothy Q. Mouse."

Dumbo crept out from under the pile of hay and stood beside Timothy Mouse, who looked him over very carefully.

"Pretty big ears, all right—" he said, almost to himself. But when he saw Dumbo look sad again he added, "But that's all right. No, it's better than all right. See, you're different from all other elephants. That's something. What if you were just like the rest of them? What would that get you? Not a thing. But you're different. You're a little elephant with big ears, so you ought to figure out something you can do that no other elephant can do. Then they'd all look up to you."

Timothy began to pace back and forth across the floor, thinking hard. Dumbo grabbed the mouse's tiny tail in his trunk and walked up and down behind him, just the way he did with his mother. Somehow, Dumbo felt safe and secure with Timothy.

"I've got it!" Timothy shouted, whirling around. "If you could just be a big success in the circus, they'd let your mother out of prison. And all the elephants would admire you, and so your mother would be happy and everything would be all right."

Dumbo nodded. Everything sounded so easy when Timothy talked about it.

"So we must figure out an act of some kind," Timothy muttered. "An act just made for you. Say—you know that big elephant balancing act right at the end of the performance?"

Dumbo nodded eagerly.

"Well," said Timothy, "just picture this. The elephants have finished building their pyramid. Then you rush out, with a flag in your trunk. See?"

Dumbo nodded again.

"You run across the ring," said Timothy Mouse, "to that springboard the acrobats use. Now remember Dumbo, the springboard is always pulled to one side of the ring before the elephant act. Well, you run and jump on the springboard and leap right up to the very top of that pile of elephants! Then you wave the flag! The audience applauds! and you're the hit of the show!"

Dumbo was very excited. But he shook his head wonderingly.

"Sure, you can do it!" cried Timothy. "I'll help you. We'll sneak out and practice at night for a while. We'll show 'em!"

With an affectionate pat on Dumbo's trunk he scampered away. Dumbo started eating the hay, paying no attention to the other elephants when they returned, still nervous and worried about the mouse. Dumbo smiled when he thought how his friend Timothy frightened them so much.

Later that night, Dumbo was sound asleep in his stall. He felt a tiny tapping against his trunk, and there was Timothy.

"Come on, Dumbo," he whispered. "We've got to practice the act."

It was not an easy job. Dumbo ran up to the springboard all right. He bounced on it hard and flew into the air. But then he lost all control. Sometimes he landed on his back, sometimes on his tail, sometimes on his trunk, sometimes on his head.

Once in a while Dumbo just bounced up and down on the springboard. He said that bouncing up and down made him feel as if he were flying. He would have liked to bounce up and down for hours, but Timothy always made him get back to work.

After several nights of practice, Dumbo improved. He could land on his feet, even when he jumped from the springboard to a stand ten feet high, then fifteen feet high, then twenty feet high.

Then Timothy decided Dumbo was ready for his big act. The next day, the performance went on as it always did. But little did the elephants or the ringmaster know what Timothy and Dumbo were planning.

Dumbo was as nervous as he could be. So much depended on his doing everything right. He clutched his little flag tightly.

The great moment finally came! The pyramid of balancing elephants was swaying in the ring. The audience was applauding loudly.

"Now!" cried Timothy.

Before he knew it, Dumbo was running toward the springboard.

THEN IT HAPPENED!

Dumbo tripped over his ears!

A gasp rose from the audience as Dumbo fell and rolled trunk over tail, trunk over tail straight for the springboard. He hurtled the length of the board, bounced into the air, and crashed right against the big ball on which the bottom elephant was balancing. The ball started to roll, and desperately the bottom elephant fought to control it while the pyramid above him swayed and rocked crazily in and out of balance.

"Run for you lives!" screamed someone in the audience, and there was a rush for the exits. Round and round, back and forth, the tottering mountain rolled. It crashed into circus apparatus, tore away ropes and poles, knocked the trapeze artists off their perches, and drove panicky clowns before it. The ringmaster tore his hair and jumped on his hat.

Little Dumbo, confused, dazed, and scarcely knowing what he was doing, stumbled after the reeling pyramid, waving his flag in his trunk with a pathetic hope that he might still get to the top.

But now the top elephant seized the center pole of the tent with his trunk. He clung to it even when it swayed and creaked and the ropes snapped. The great tent sagged and then, with a crash, the pole toppled to the ground and the whole structure gave way. Amid yells and screams and roars and bellows, the tent settled to the ground.

From the wreckage, the trunk of a little elephant waved a tiny flag.

It was night. Casey Jr. had pulled the circus train out of town far behind schedule because of the wreck caused by Dumbo's fall, which had disgraced the entire circus.

The elephant car looked like a hospital. Old Rajah stood with a sling supporting his heavily bandaged trunk. "Sixty years I've been in the circus," he moaned, "but never have I seen anything like that."

Another elephant with big lumps on his head cried, "Yes, and it was that ridiculous little son of Mrs. Jumbo that did it, too."

"He's a disgrace to our race," said another elephant. "I think we should disown him."

"Yes! You're right!" they all cried.

"It's a real shame," Old Rajah said to the elephants. "But I suppose it's the only thing to do. We can't ever admit to anyone that an elephant became a clown."

"A clown?" gasped others in horror.

"Yes, that's his punishment," Rajah said. "The ringmaster has decided to turn him over to the clowns."

The elephants all agreed that this was indeed the worst punishment that could have been found for an elephant.

At the next town the circus equipment was repaired and the clowns prepared for their new act with Dumbo. They fastened a bright yellow ruff around his neck. They powdered his head a clownish white, and on his sad face they painted a big crimson grin. A pointed dunce cap topped off the silly make-up.

Dumbo was the saddest little elephant in the whole world.

Oh, it was fine for the crowds, who had never seen anything so funny. It was fine for the ringmaster, who at last could figure on some profit from his ridiculous little elephant. It was fine for everyone but Dumbo, who cried himself to sleep every night, and for his mother, who wanted more than ever to be with her little son to comfort him and care for him, and for Timothy, who felt that

DISNEY G.S. BK—C

it was really all his fault because his idea had turned out so badly.

Timothy tried to smile and make Dumbo feel good. He said he would have another idea, a better one that would surely work. But he knew the clowns would never let Dumbo go, that no one would ever give him a chance again.

The new act was the hit of the show. The clowns built, right in the middle of the big tent, a three-story building. Of course, it was only a false front, like a movie set. Suddenly flames and smoke belched from the windows and the clowns rushed in dressed like firemen. Their buckets were sieves and their hoses squirted just a drop of water at a time, and the audience roared at their antics.

Suddenly, at the topmost window, Dumbo appeared. Wearing a golden wig and dressed in a pink nightgown, he was frantically waving a white handkerchief in his trunk. A clown rushed into the tent—crying to the firemen to save her darling child. The fire fighters brought out a large round safety net and cried, "Jump! Jump!"

Then Dumbo jumped. Down, down, down he hurtled as the crowd howled in excitement. Dumbo hit the net hard—and crashed right through it, landing in a large tub of white plaster underneath.

The audience roared with laughter and the clowns took their bows. It was the biggest success of the circus!

Yes, Dumbo was now the great climax of a big success. But it brought him no happiness. He trudged out of the tent, dripping wet plaster behind him, having fun poked at him all the way. As he passed the other elephants they turned their backs to him, and even the monkeys looked the other way.

But back in his stall there was Timothy. Timothy was smiling bravely, telling Dumbo there was still a little plaster behind his ears as he washed himself, trying to make jokes and see Dumbo laugh. But it was no use. Dumbo wouldn't smile. He wouldn't eat, even when Timothy brought him a few peanuts he had saved for him.

Timothy did not know what to say as they settled down to sleep. He climbed up Dumbo's trunk and found a comfortable bed in the brim of Dumbo's little pointed hat.

"Dumbo," he said.

Dumbo just nodded slowly to show Timothy he was listening.

"Dumbo, I'm going to figure out something so that this clown business stops, so your mother will be free, and so you'll be a success. Now just go to sleep and stop worrying. Pretty soon you'll be a great success, you'll be happy, you'll be flying high!"

Dumbo smiled. Timothy was a good friend, even if his ideas didn't work. He dropped off to sleep, smiling over Timothy's idea that soon he would be flying high. That reminded him of the times he used to jump from the springboard. How good that felt!

Dumbo fell asleep, dreaming of that one great chance, which had turned into such failure, and now in his dream it became a great success. He waited at the entrance, sped gracefully toward the springboard, and bounced high into the air. Up and up he soared, gliding into the air with such ease that it seemed no effort at all.

It was a wonderful dream, and it seemed very real to Dumbo.

The morning sun rose on a perfectly natural landscape. There were trees and grass and a brook and a road. But there was something wrong about the scene. It was not at all according to Nature or Nature's laws that a certain tree should bear, high up in its branches, the form of a sleeping elephant.

The elephant was comfortably cradled in a forked limb, lying on its back with its ears and legs dangling loosely. The ears were unmistakable. It was Dumbo! And in the brim of his hat lay Timothy, still sleeping soundly.

A noisy group of birds had gathered around them, chattering their disapproval and scolding shrilly. Timothy stirred, disturbed by the insistent racket, and opened his eyes sleepily. He blinked, and a pair of eyes not a foot away blinked right back at him. A large, rusty-looking crow, evidently the leader of the birds, was glaring at him sternly. Timothy shifted uncomfortably.

"What are you doing down here?" he finally asked irritably.

"What are *you* doing up *here?*" the crow snapped back.

"Oh, go away!" said Timothy, who didn't like to be bothered before he was fully awake. He closed his eyes and settled down for another nap, since Dumbo was still asleep. "I'm here because I belong here," he muttered to the crow. "I live here!"

"So do we!" cawed the crow.

This made Timothy blink again.

"Oh, stop talking nonsense," Timothy said. "Run along and mind your own business."

"Haw!" cawed the crow loudly. "That's good! I suppose it's not my business when an elephant comes flying in here at midnight! And it's not my business when you knock my nest to pieces and scare my whole family out of their feather beds! Say, do you have any idea where you are?"

"Sure," replied Timothy, rubbing his eyes. "I'm right where I belong, in the circus. And what are you and your friends doing around this tent, I'd like to know."

Screams of laughter burst from the circle of birds. Timothy sat bolt upright and peered down to look at Dumbo, whose eyelids were beginning to flicker. Then he gazed at the canopy of leaves overhead, the trunk, the bark, and the branches of what certainly was a tree. And then he looked down—far, far down—at the ground.

They really *were* up in a tree!

"Dumbo!" he cried. "Dumbo! Take a look down—down there!" But just as Dumbo, who was still sprawled out on his back, started to turn his head, Timothy thought better of it. "NO, DON'T! DON'T LOOK!"

Dumbo had already glanced down. For one long minute he looked. Then he scrambled to his feet. Trying to balance in the wobbly fork of the tree, he teetered back and forth like a tightrope walker in a high wind.

Dumbo lost his hold and fell to the branch below. Timothy clutched the elephant's hat brim and shut his eyes. The second branch broke, and Dumbo fell. He clutched at the lowest branch, and it seemed that it might save him. But elephants were never meant to cling to branches. Dumbo fell!

He landed in a shallow brook that flowed under the tree, and Timothy fell into the water beside him. Dripping wet, the two sat in the stream while raucous shouts of laughter poured down on them.

"Now, try to keep your feet on the ground," cawed one crow. "It's not right for elephants to fly."

Dumbo and Timothy picked themselves up without a word and trudged off into the woods. They were bewildered and confused. Where were they? Dumbo could not imagine what had happened.

Timothy was speechless. He plodded along, hands clasped behind his back, his face a mask of puzzlement. Thoughts popped in his mind like firecrackers. "It's not right for elephants to fly? I wonder what that old crow meant. How did we ever get up into that tree? Dumbo can't fly. He hasn't got any wings. The only thing he has are those big—*say*, that gives me an idea!"

He stopped and turned to Dumbo. "Did you fly last night?"

Dumbo shook his head and smiled at Timothy as if he were a little crazy. Then he stopped with a startled expression.

"What is it?" Timothy asked impatiently. "Come on, tell me!"

Dumbo told Timothy Mouse about his dream the night before—how he had jumped on the springboard, sailed into the air, and flown away.

"If dreams could only come true, Dumbo!" Timothy said. "Well, I guess there's nothing to that flying idea."

They walked on aimlessly. But the same thought kept running through Timothy's head. "We got up into that tree somehow, dream or no dream. And people have walked in their sleep—so why couldn't they fly in their sleep?"

Timothy Mouse stopped and put his hands on his hips. "That just must be the answer! Dumbo flew in his sleep, and that's how we got up in that tree. And if Dumbo hasn't got wings, then the only thing he could fly with are his ears!"

He turned to Dumbo. "Listen, Dumbo. You can fly. You were right! You flew last night. You are going to fly again! Come on over here and we'll practice."

Dumbo followed Timothy obediently. But he remembered the many bad falls he had taken when he practiced on the springboard, and he remembered how that idea had finally turned out. This would be even worse. But he could think of nothing else to do, so he put himself in Timothy's hands.

In the field, they set to work. Timothy told Dumbo to flap his ears up and down vigorously, going faster and faster.

"One! Two! One! Two! Up! Down! Up! Down! Faster! Faster!" Timothy Mouse shouted at the little elephant.

Dumbo flapped his ears in time and a cloud of dust arose around them. Birds and small animals of the woods gathered around this strange sight in curious wonder. Then the flapping became slower and slower and ceased altogether, and out of the dust staggered the two grimy and choking partners.

From the trees around them came a chorus of laughs and jeers from their audience, chiefly from the crows who had followed them through the woods.

"Get a balloon!" shrieked the leader of the crows, and the others cackled loudly.

Timothy Mouse gritted his teeth, pulled his hat way down over his ears, and began with Dumbo again.

Dumbo galloped in a circle, and about every fifth step his flapping ears lifted him off the ground a few inches. The birds thought this was the funniest thing they'd ever seen, and they fluttered along beside him, imitating his clumsy efforts. Dumbo, confused and excited, didn't look where he was going and ran into a tree. He lay sprawled on the ground while the birds gathered round and jeered.

"Happy landings!" the big crow cackled, and the other crows cawed their approval. Even Dumbo thought it was funny, much to Timothy's disgust.

"Don't pay any attention to them," he said to Dumbo. "They probably laughed at the Wright brothers, too. You're doing fine. Now let's go over to this little hill and take off from there."

Dumbo took off from the little hill, all right, but he landed, too—in a mudhole. And Timothy, who made the trip in Dumbo's hat, bore his share of the crack-up.

The crows followed Timothy and Dumbo and laughed louder than ever.

Timothy could stand it no longer.

"Wait a minute!" Timothy shouted at them in a voice hoarse with rage.

The birds cocked their heads wonderingly.

"I want to ask you something. Is there a single one among you who has a heart?"

Timothy looked around at them all. The little mouse stared at them hard in the sudden silence. They all felt a little embarrassed.

"If there is," the mouse went on, more calmly, "I want to tell you a sad story. I want to tell you about somebody who had the misfortune of being born different from others—somebody who, just because he *was* different, and through no fault of his own, brought sorrow to himself and his poor old mother. This little fellow tried to hold his head up and smile, to be a success. But then came the cruelest blow of all. They made him a CLOWN!"

A chorus of sympathetic noises came from the birds and animals.

Then Timothy drove home his point.

"Here I am trying to help my friend Dumbo be a success, and what do *you* do? You sit on your perches and laugh at us—yes, you laugh at us!"

The birds hung their heads guiltily. There was a silence, and then the big crow spoke.

"Well, you see," he said apologetically, "we didn't understand. We'll do whatever we can to help, won't we fellows?"

There was a loud cawing of approval as the birds flew down and gathered around Dumbo and Timothy.

The old crow took Timothy to one side. "Listen," he said, "the only reason Dumbo can't fly is that he hasn't any confidence. He just thinks he can't. We have the same trouble with our young ones. They don't want to try it at first, either. They're scared when they look out of the nest. So we give them a feather—any old feather—and tell them it's a magic feather from Persia and that anyone who holds it in his beak can fly. It always works. Here's a feather. Go on Timothy—try it on Dumbo."

Timothy took the feather from the old crow and ran joyfully back to Dumbo. The little elephant looked doubtful, but Timothy was so happy, so certain, so confident, that he began to believe him. When he took the feather in his trunk, he seemed to feel a new strength flowing into him.

Timothy climbed into Dumbo's hat, and the little elephant scampered up the hill once more. The birds gathered around expectantly, no longer making fun. There was silence as Dumbo stood on the crest of the hill and began to flap his ears. He closed his eyes, clutched the magic feather, and flapped his ears faster and faster.

Timothy held on to his hat. He closed his eyes to keep out the dust. He could not see a thing, but then he felt Dumbo moving beneath him. Then, as the dust cleared away, he looked over the brim of the hat. Dumbo was FLYING!

"Look, Dumbo, look!" Timothy shouted, and for the first time Dumbo opened his eyes. When he saw himself heading for a treetop, he almost fainted and fell, but he clutched the feather, flapped his ears, and banked gently in a curve around the tree. The crows flew around him, cheering encouragingly. Dumbo flew more and more gracefully, sailing through the air with ease.

It was wonderful! It was even more wonderful than his dream!

Slowly he leveled off to come to a landing. For his first attempt, it was pretty good. He bumped a little and nosed over on his trunk, spilling Timothy out on the ground. But the two partners did not mind at all. They got up laughing and shouting with glee as the birds circled around them, cawing their applause.

For the next few hours, Dumbo practiced. The crows taught him how to bank and turn and soar and glide and loop. In a short while Dumbo was making smooth three-point landings every time.

Timothy now saw that the sun was sinking; it was late.

"Say, we must be getting back to the circus," he said to Dumbo. "We're going to surprise them in that show tonight. We'll have to think of some story to explain where we've been all day."

The old crow told them how to get to the circus grounds, a few miles away, and with a dipping salute to his friends the crows, Dumbo flew away.

Timothy made him land on the edge of town and walk into the circus grounds. He had a carefully laid plan for the evening performance, and he didn't want Dumbo to give away their secret until exactly the right moment. Dumbo promised not to say a word.

And so the two partners came back home to the circus. Timothy scampered off to his house under the ringmaster's tent, and Dumbo brought joy to the clowns by his return. They had been afraid that the funny animal which was the climax of their act had disappeared forever.

Dumbo sat patiently while the clowns put on his make-up and his costume for the evening performance. And when the time came for him to climb up behind the window of the fake building, Timothy joined him and jumped into his hat.

"Our big moment has come, Dumbo!" Timothy whispered excitedly. "Just wait until after this act, and the whole world will be eating out of our hands."

Dumbo just nodded and smiled. Inside he was trembling, but he tried to act calm and serene. He didn't want Timothy to know that he was afraid. Dumbo looked confidently at the little black feather, which he clutched in the end of his trunk.

The clown act began. Smoke and flames poured from the windows of the building. The clowns rushed in with their sieve-buckets and waterless hoses. Dumbo stood at the window, the spotlight on him. Below he saw the clowns with the life-saving net spread out above the tub of wet plaster.

No more plaster for him! he thought. And he jumped. But at that moment, the black feather slipped from his trunk and floated away. Dumbo stared in horror, and his heart sank in fear. Was he to fail once again?

Timothy saw the feather go, too, and realized what effect this would have on Dumbo. As they plunged down, down, toward the ground, Timothy shouted to Dumbo, pleading with him to spread his ears and fly. But Dumbo seemed not to hear. He had closed his eyes and decided that once more his high hopes would be dashed. In a flash, Timothy jumped from the hat and holding on tightly, scampered down Dumbo's trunk and looked him in the eye.

"Dumbo!" he shouted frantically. "Dumbo! You *can* fly! That feather didn't mean a thing. It was fake. You can fly without it. You *can* fly! *You can fly!*"

Timothy's insistent words reached Dumbo's ears. He opened his eyes and saw the firemen's net just below him. "YOU CAN FLY!" screamed Timothy, as Dumbo spread his ears wide and swooped up into the air when he was not two feet above the net!

One mighty gasp arose from the great audience! They rubbed their eyes! They pinched themselves! They knew it couldn't be, but it was happening!

Dumbo was flying!

Timothy, who had braced himself for the crash, slowly opened his eyes and pulled himself back up to the hat brim. When he got his breath back, he looked over the edge and gloried in the sight of the wildly applauding crowd below him.

"Dumbo, you're wonderful!" he shouted. "Marvelous! The greatest thing on earth! Dumbo, look at them shouting for you! The audience is shouting for you, Dumbo!"

Dumbo swooped up to the highest point

in the tent and then plunged down, down, DOWN, and not until the very last instant did he level off and sail gently over the heads of the audience, which was in a state of utter collapse from the sheer excitement of it all.

Then Dumbo repeated his power dive. He flew upside down, barrel-rolled back to level flight, and did loops, spins, and falling leaves. He swooped down to pick up peanuts and squirted a trunkful of water on the clowns. The crowd roared.

The news spread like wildfire. The town was aroused and came rushing to the circus. All the animals in the circus, too, heard what was going on. And the animal keepers quickly brought Mrs. Jumbo from her prison car so she could watch her son thrilling the crowds. Dumbo dipped in salute to her as she came into the tent, and the crowd roared its applause for the mother of this flying marvel.

Dumbo flew for a full hour, and when he finally came to a beautiful landing by the

side of his mother, everyone was exhausted from the excitement, hoarse from shouting. With dignity, Dumbo escorted his mother to their stall, as Timothy held back the crowds that surged around.

"Stand back, everyone," he shouted. "Give the star a chance to rest. Give the great Dumbo, the Flying Elephant, an opportunity to have a little time alone with his dear mother. No conferences until tomorrow morning," cried Timothy Mouse.

And so Timothy became Dumbo's manager. And he saw to it that Dumbo got a wonderful contract, with a big salary, a pension for his mother, and a special streamlined car on the circus train. Dumbo flew in great aviation contests, made a good-will tour of South America, broke all altitude records, and helped the Army and Navy in their aviation training programs.

And through it all he remained the simple, kind little fellow that he had always been. He didn't forget his old friends the crows, who frequently went on private flying parties with him. He bought some shiny new whistles for Casey Jr. He saw to it that Timothy had always on hand a supply of every known type of cheese.

And now, as the circus train puffed across the country, Casey Jr. tooted his bright new whistles happily. In the elephant car, the big elephants stood on boxes, flapping their ears.

They jumped, hoping they would fly even a few feet. But each one of them crashed and gave up.

At last all the elephants, even Old Rajah, agreed that there could be only one Dumbo, the Flying Elephant.

In the special streamlined car at the rear of the train Dumbo sat snuggled close to his mother, Mrs. Jumbo, whose trunk was curled about him affectionately. Nearby sat Timothy Mouse contentedly humming a tune.

Thus the circus train with "Dumbo's Flying Circus" sped across the country toward the bright lights of Hollywood, where new triumphs awaited Timothy Mouse and Dumbo, the one and only Flying Elephant.

ALICE IN WONDERLAND MEETS THE WHITE RABBIT

Do you know where Wonderland is? It is the place you visit in your dreams, the strange and wondrous place where nothing is as it seems. It was in Wonderland that Alice met the White Rabbit.

He was hurrying across the meadow, looking at his pocket watch and saying to himself: "I'm late, I'm late, for a very important date.

"I'm in a rabbit stew, oh oh! Can't even say good-bye—hello! I'm late, I'm late, I'm late!"

He hopped across the brook and disappeared into a hollow tree.

"That's curious," said Alice. "A rabbit who wears a waistcoat, and carries a watch, and can talk!

"He's in such a hurry, he must be going to a party. I surely would like to go, too."

So Alice followed him.

"What a peculiar place to give a party," she thought as she pushed her way into the hollow tree.

But before she could think any more, she began to slide on some slippery white pebbles inside. And then she began to fall!

"Curious and curiouser!" said Alice as she floated slowly down, past cupboards and lamps, a rocking chair, past clocks and mirrors she met in mid-air.

By the time she reached the bottom the White Rabbit was disappearing through a little door. The door was much too small for Alice to follow him.

Poor Alice! She was all alone in Wonderland, where nothing was just what it seemed. (You know how things are in dreams!)

Whenever she ate a bite of cake or took a sip to drink, she would shoot up tall or grow so tiny she was sometimes afraid she would vanish quite away.

She met other animals, yes, indeed, strange talking animals, too. They tried to be as helpful as they could. But they couldn't help her find the White Rabbit.

"And I really must find him," Alice thought, though she wasn't sure just why.

So on she wandered through Wonderland, all by her lonely self.

At last she reached a neat little house in the woods, with pink shutters and a little front door that opened and—out came the White Rabbit!

"Oh, my twitching whiskers!" he was saying to himself. He seemed very much upset. Then he looked up and saw Alice standing there.

"Mary Ann!" he said sharply. "Why, Mary Ann, what are you doing here? Well, don't just do something, stand there! No, go get my gloves. I'm very late!"

"But late for what?" Alice began to ask.

"My gloves!" said the White Rabbit firmly. And Alice dutifully went to look for them, though she knew she wasn't Mary Ann!

When she came back, the White Rabbit was just disappearing through the woods again.

So off went Alice, trying to follow him through that strange, mixed-up Wonderland.

She met Tweedledee and Tweedledum, a funny little pair.

She joined a mad tea party with the Mad Hatter and the March Hare.

48

She met a Cheshire cat who faded in and out of sight. And one strange creature—Jabberwock—whose eyes flamed in the night.

They all were very kind, but they could not show Alice the way, until:

"There *is* a short cut," she heard the Cheshire cat say. So Alice took it.

The short cut led into a garden where gardeners were busy painting roses red.

"We must hurry," they said, "for the Queen is coming!"

And sure enough, a trumpet blew, and a voice called:

"Make way for the Queen of Hearts!"

Then out came a grand procession. And who should be the royal trumpeter for the cross-looking Queen but the White Rabbit.

"Well!" said Alice. "So this is why he was hurrying so!"

"Who are you?" snapped the Queen. "Do you play croquet?"

"I'm Alice. And I'm just on my way home. Thank you for the invitation, but I really mustn't stay."

"So!" cried the Queen. "So she won't play! Off with her head then!"

But Alice was tired of Wonderland now, and all its nonsensical ways.

"Pooh!" she said. "I'm not frightened of you. You're nothing but a pack of cards."

And with that she ran back through that land of dreams, back to the river bank where she had fallen asleep.

"Hm," she said, as she rubbed her eyes. "I'm glad to be back where things are what they seem. I've had quite enough for now of Wonderland!"

DONALD DUCK
IN DISNEYLAND

"Hurry up, boys. Keep together. And stay right with me," said Donald Duck anxiously as he and his nephews moved along with the crowd toward the gates of Disneyland.

Soon they found themselves in the railroad station entrance to Disneyland. Beyond the open doorway stretched Main Street, U.S.A.

And beyond that, as the boys well knew, spread a magic wonder world.

"Come on!" cried Huey, tugging at Donald.

"Let's go to Fantasyland!" cried Dewey.

"No, the World of Tomorrow!" said Louie.

"Rocket to the Moon!" Huey broke in.

"Wait!" said Donald. "First we must take the train ride around Disneyland and see the overall view." So he bought four tickets.

But when he turned around, not a single nephew was in sight.

"Train ride's a perfect way to spot lost boys," the train conductor suggested.

So Donald hopped aboard and found himself a seat. The train started up and soon was steaming past the tropical jungles of True-Life Adventure Land.

As Donald watched, dazzled by the bright flowers and brilliant birds in the trees, a river boat chugged into view. And there at the rail lounged Huey Duck.

But Huey could not see an alligator which was waiting just about the bend, with wide and grinning jaws.

"Watch out, Huey!" Donald cried, but the train chugged out of sight before the boat reached the bend. "Stop the train!" cried Donald. "I have to get out!" But the train went chugging on.

51

Ahead a whistle hooted. Donald looked around. The scenery had changed. Here a paddle-wheel excursion boat was steaming down A River of America, and on the far bank sprawled a quaint old river town.

Donald scanned the steamer's decks. Just then the steam whistle screeched *toot-a-toot toot!* And there, hanging on the whistle cord, was grinning Dewey Duck!

Around a curve in a desert road, a stagecoach came lurching at full speed.

At the window of the stagecoach two faces appeared—surely Huey and Louie Duck!

Just behind it raced wild Indians, waving bows and tomahawks, and shrieking war cries.

"Down, boys!" shouted Donald as the train raced past. "Get out of their range!"

"Toot toot! Down below ran another train, the *Casey, Jr.,* on a dizzy ride. And in the cab of the engineer, whom should Donald

spy but Dewey Duck, waving to Uncle Donald.

"Keep your eyes on the track!" shouted Uncle Donald. "Watch where you're taking the train!"

As Donald sank trembling into his seat, down the aisle the jolly conductor came.

"No sign of your nephews yet?" he smiled. "Well, don't you worry. They'll turn up safe and sound." With a pat on Donald's shoulder, he went on his way.

"Turn up!" Donald gasped. "Safe and sound!" He shuddered.

For a few moments then the train chugged past a green and shady grove. Donald stretched and took a deep, happy breath. Everything looked so peaceful here.

"Whee! Look at me, Unca Donald!" cried a familiar voice.

Donald spun around.

A pirate ship was sailing toward the clouds, on its way to Peter Pan's Neverland.

From the deck Louie Duck waved both hands at Uncle Don. But far ahead Donald could see Captain Hook with drawn sword, waiting for the ship to come near.

"Get your head down and hang on tight!" called Donald. But Louie had not heard. As he disappeared, he was waving still.

"Some fun, Unca Donald. Look at me!"

Down a streamlined highway small cars were running—an intent young driver at each wheel. In one car was Huey Duck, steering with both hands.

"Huey! You don't know how to drive!" called Donald, not knowing that Huey had just passed his Disneyland Driving Test. Then the train took Donald out of sight; and to his relief he saw the station ahead.

Donald was the first one off the train. But his shaking knees would not take him far. He had to stop and lean against a post, one hand over his eyes. Where, he wondered, was the hospital? He supposed he should look there first.

"Unca Donald!" "Hurry up!" "The train's about to leave!" Huey, Dewey, and Louie were dancing around him.

"We've had a wonderful time!" they said. "Now we're ready to go with you for a quiet trip on the train."

"Quiet!" squeaked Donald. "You boys go ahead. I can't stand that excitement again."

So while the boys hopped onto the train, Donald tottered off to take a peaceful rocket trip to the moon.

WALT DISNEY'S THE SWORD IN THE STONE

ONCE IN old England there lived a nobleman who had two boys of whom he was very fond. Sir Ector was his name.

Kay, the elder boy, was of great size and strength of bone. He was also stubborn and lazy, but he was the nobleman's own son. When he grew older he would be Sir Kay and master of the castle.

The younger boy was called Wart. He was an adopted son, and could not hope to become a knight. Nevertheless the scrawny little fellow was full of smiles, and not one bit jealous of Kay.

One day Wart merrily followed Kay to a forest's edge. To keep out of the way there, Wart climbed a tree while Kay fitted a bow to an arrow and took aim at a deer. Kay aimed true, but just then there was a great cracking sound. It was the tree branch breaking under Wart's weight.

Startled, Kay released the arrow too quickly. It flew wide of the deer and disappeared into the forest. Watching it vanish, Kay shook with rage.

"Oh, please, Kay. I'm sorry," cried Wart. "I'll get it for you."

And he ran to search for the arrow in the forest, a dark and perilous place.

The perilous forest was no different from the rest of England in those days. Many years before, so long ago that Wart could not even remember it, good King Uther had ruled the land wisely and well. But when Uther died, he left no heir to the throne.

After Uther's death all the lords and nobles came to the greatest church in London Town to see if God would show them who should be king. There a wondrous thing happened. Suddenly a huge marble stone appeared in the churchyard, and, on the stone there was a steel anvil. Thrust through the anvil, deep into the stone, was a sword with these words written in gold below the hilt.

WHOSO PULLETH OUT THIS SWORD OF THIS STONE AND ANVIL IS RIGHTWISE KING BORN OF ENGLAND.

Though the lords and nobles tried with all their strength, none could stir the sword. So England was still without a king. The realm fell into great disorder and the strong preyed upon the weak.

In time the miracle of the sword was forgotten. Weeds sprang up around the anvil, and vines covered the sword, just as they grew wild in the forest.

And now Wart was deep inside the gloomy forest, fighting his way step by step through the tangled underbrush. He ventured on bravely, tripping over countless roots and having his face lashed by countless brambles. At last he came to a tiny clearing in the very heart of the forest.

In the clearing stood a snug little cottage with a thatched roof. A tree that grew close to the cottage stretched its branches so low down that some of them almost touched the roof. And there was the lost arrow, caught in among those branches. Wart stared openmouthed, amazed at his good fortune.

He neither saw nor heard the fierce wolf ready to spring at him.

The wolf rushed out, growling fiercely. He sprang, but his jaws clashed shut on empty air. For Wart, eager to recover the arrow, had scrambled up the tree just in time.

As Wart climbed up, leaves closed around him on all sides. The wolf was hidden from his view as it prowled around the base of the tree, hoping he might fall.

Peering about, Wart saw the arrow at the far end of a spreading branch. Without another thought he went out towards it.

The branch had begun to bend and creak when at last he had his hand on the arrow. Then it happened. With a great cracking sound a tree branch broke under his weight for the second time that day.

Down fell Wart, head over heels, through the thatched roof.

Wart landed with a thump in front of a table neatly set for tea. "So you did drop in," said a calm voice. "But you are a bit late, you know."

"I—I am?" stammered Wart. He stared across the table at an old gentleman in a strange, pointed hat and a flowing gown.

"My name is Merlin," said the old gentleman. "Come lad, what is your name?"

"My name is Arthur, but everyone calls me Wart."

"Ah!" said Merlin. "Will you have your tea now, Wart?"

Before Wart could answer there was a rustle of soft wings, and an owl rose from his perch near the table and flew across the room.

"Oh!" cried Wart in surprise. "I thought that owl was stuffed."

"Who's stuffed?" said the owl, deeply insulted. "Who? Who?"

"It talks!" cried Wart.

"His name is Archimedes," said Merlin. "He is a highly educated owl."

"I am sorry I mistook you for a stuffed owl," Wart told Archimedes, and from that time on the owl was his friend.

"Sir," Wart said to Merlin, as they drank their tea, "would you mind if I asked you a question? How did you know I would be—?"

"That you would be dropping in?" interrupted Merlin. "Well you see, my boy, I happen to be a wizard."

Wart was very surprised. He had never met a wizard.

"I can see into the future," said Merlin. "Centuries into the future. I have even been there."

"Do you mean that you know everything before it happens?" asked Wart.

"Not everything," said Merlin. "But this I do know—fate has directed you to me so that I may guide you to your rightful place in the world. I am going to be your tutor."

"But I have to get back to the castle!" cried Wart.

"Very well," said Merlin. He stood up and, waving his wand at the four corners of the cottage, he commanded, "Pack up!"

At this all of Merlin's belongings—tables, chairs, chests, china, cutlery, cauldrons, glass retorts, bottles, brooms, benches, and books by the thousands—rose up into the air. There was a great roaring and a hissing noise as the things swirled round and round and got smaller and smaller. When they were small enough they flew into a small leather suitcase standing by the door. The suitcase snapped shut and locked itself securely. And then there was utter silence.

"Come, boy," said Merlin. "I'm going with you to your castle, and it's high time we got started."

Sir Ector let out a loud bellow when he saw Wart enter the great hall of the castle. Although he was very fond of the boy, worry had set the nobleman raging.

"What's the idea of barging off in that infernal forest alone!" he roared. "For that you'll get four hours extra kitchen duty! Report to the cook—hop it, boy! Hop, hop, hop it!"

As Wart scurried off to the kitchen, Merlin greeted Sir Ector and told him why he had come to the castle with his owl and his suitcase.

"Gadzooks!" roared the nobleman. "I'm the one to decide whether or not Wart is getting a proper education!" Then, with a snort, he asked, "Who are you?"

"My name is Merlin," said Merlin, drawing himself up proudly. "And I happen to be the world's most powerful wizard."

Thinking he was dealing with an addled old man, Sir Ector began to laugh at Merlin.

"Hoo-hoo!" he laughed heartily. "The world's most powerful wizard—what a joke!"

"Snow," said Merlin.

Immediately enormous white flakes began to float about in the great hall.

Sir Ector blinked his eyes, then he said, "I know that trick. It's done with mirrors."

"Snow harder," said Merlin.

At once a wintry blast blew through the hall, and the flakes grew bigger and bigger. In an instant Sir Ector's nose was blue with cold and he stood up to his knees in a snow drift.

"That—that's enough," he cried hastily through chattering teeth. "You're welcome to stay, if you like."

The snow stopped immediately.

"You can stay in the northwest tower," cried Sir Ector. "That's the guest room. Just —just make yourself at home."

Merlin smiled and said, "You're very generous."

With the owl flying ahead of him, and the suitcase floating along behind, the old wizard started the long, slow climb up the tower staircase.

Down in the great hall Sir Ector snorted with glee. "Just wait till Merlin sees that guest room—he won't stay here more than two days!"

The guest room in the northwest tower was drafty when the wind blew, and it leaked like a waterspout when it rained. When the owl saw it he wanted to leave at once.

But Merlin said, "This may be a room for unwelcome guests, but we will stay. For Wart has a future, and he must have an education."

"Future!" cried the owl in a bitter voice. "What kind of future can that scrawny little orphan boy have? Tell me that."

"Don't be rude, Archimedes," said Merlin, suddenly stern, "or I'll turn you into a human."

"Oh you wouldn't!" cried Archimedes.

And that was that. They stayed.

One day they saw a knight come galloping into the courtyard far below their tower. From the outcry it was plain to see that he was the bearer of important news. So Merlin sent the owl down to find out what it was.

Sir Ector welcomed the knight and led him into the great hall. With a flip of his wings the owl flew in after them.

The knight cleared his throat and said, "On New Year's Day in London Town there will be a tournament."

"Oh?" said Sir Ector, yawning.

"The winner of the tournament," the knight continued, "will be crowned king of all England."

"What!" cried Sir Ector, leaping up excitedly. And turning to his boys he said, "Kay, lad, did you hear that? You could win it, if you knuckle down to your training. We'll have you knighted by Christmas and off to London.

"And Wart—you will go as Kay's squire."

After flying back with the news, the owl sat quietly and wondered. *Why hold a tournament to choose the king? Isn't there some sort of sword . . . ?*

Merlin said, "If you're thinking of the Sword in the Stone—that is long forgotten."

Days passed, with Sir Ector always watching closely over Kay's training program. There were extra lessons from dawn to dusk, and Kay grumbled without a stop, for now he had no time for his favorite sport, which was to stretch out lazily in the sun.

One day he put on a heavy suit of armor and mounted a horse in order to take a jousting lesson. Grumbling through his visor, Kay held the lance directly forward and charged the practice machine. Wart, who was cranking the machine, flinched as the thumping of the horse's iron hoofs came closer and closer.

The machine spun around with great rapidity, and its spear swept Kay out of his saddle.

"Help!" he cried, flying through the air.

Clang! went his armor as Kay hit a stone wall.

For the rest of that day he lay stretched out in the sun.

"Wart," said Merlin one blazing hot day, "I think it is about time I began *your* lessons." And leading the boy out to the castle moat, he said, "Can you imagine what it is like to be a fish?"

"That's easy," said Wart. "I've done it lots of times."

Merlin waved his wand and said a magic word.

Immediately Wart tumbled off the bank and landed with a splash in the moat.

He had turned into a perch, which is a very small fish. A moment later Merlin, too, had changed into a fish—a graying, elderly trout.

"You are a fish," said Merlin. "But you are not used to being a fish. So you will have to use your head, little perch."

Trying to obey, Wart learned how to swim like a perch.

Suddenly a monstrous pike loomed up and hungrily opened its mouth.

"Merlin!" cried Wart. "Help me! Use magic!"

But Merlin was so startled that he could not think of the magic words that could save Wart. "You must help yourself," he cried. Off darted Wart—and the chase was on!

The pike came closer and closer, its giant body almost invisible in the shadowy murk. With a cunning flick of his tail, Wart vanished altogether behind a clump of weed.

The pike slowly nosed its way into the grassy tangle. Thinking quickly, Wart shot up and did a series of jack-knives that took him high above the water.

The pike was leaping savagely after him when something unexpected happened. There was a sudden rushing noise and, in mid-air, a little claw snatched Wart out of harm's way. It was Archimedes. The owl had come swooping down in the nick of time.

Immediately Wart was a boy again and standing on dry land.

"Well done," said Merlin. "You outwitted that big brute this time!"

As a tiny perch Wart had learned to use his brains. He knew that size and strength weren't the most important things. Now the days passed swiftly, and his education went on.

"I think it is time," said Merlin to him one afternoon, "that you had another lesson."

"Oh, no, sir," said Wart, who was working by himself in the castle kitchen. "I'd better not. I have all this work to do."

Merlin smiled. With a wave of his hand he said, "Clean up."

At once all the dishes that were heaped around, ready to be washed, floated into the air, formed an orderly line and danced over to an enormous bucket of soapy water. A brush and a dishcloth came to life and briskly scrubbed the dishes. Brooms whisked over flagstones while mops sloshed round and round.

"Well," said Merlin, urging Wart towards the door, "a little magic certainly goes a long way, doesn't it? Come, boy, it's time to start your lesson."

But while they were gone, the cook, who had been napping, returned to the kitchen.

And then Merlin's magic went even further than he had expected.

At the sight of dishes washing themselves, brooms sweeping flagstones with no human hands to guide them, and mops sloshing round and round the self-same way—the cook began to shriek.

Hearing her shrieks, Sir Ector and Kay came rushing in, bravely brandishing swords.

Shouting "To the rescue!" and "Take that!" Sir Ector charged at the lively line of dishes. But after a few steps, he skidded on the wet floor. His arms flailing wildly, the nobleman went sliding over to the enormous bucket. With a great splash he fell in.

The dishcloth and the brush scrubbed Sir Ector with great vigor. Meanwhile all over

the kitchen brooms still swept flagstones and mops sloshed round and round.

At that moment Wart walked in.

Shaking his fist at the poor boy, Sir Ector roared furiously, "Blast it, Wart! It's all your fault! You brought Merlin here. Just for this —you won't even be Kay's squire!"

A few days later Wart was still downcast. "I can't even hope to be a squire," he told Merlin mournfully. "What's the use of another lesson?"

Merlin chucked him under the chin and said, "You mustn't give up. Come, lad, smile, now."

Wart saw a bird flash by the tower window. With a sigh he said, "I'm tired of being Wart. I wish I were a bird."

In an instant he was a little sparrow.

Archimedes taught Wart to use his wings. They were flying along far from the castle when they were sighted by a hungry hawk.

At once the bird of prey plummeted down at them, its talons pointing directly at the little sparrow.

"Hawk!" cried the owl, terribly alarmed. "Wart, look out!"

With a flick of his wings, Wart darted away. But the hawk followed him, its huge black wings beating strongly.

It was a long and terrible chase, far beyond the strength of a feeble sparrow. Wart, however, escaped the hawk's cruel talons by dropping down a chimney. With the lightest of thumps he fell to the bottom of a cold and cobwebby fireplace.

A gnarled hand lifted him.

A cackling voice said, "Well, look who came to visit me—a scrawny little sparrow with a beakful of soot."

It was Madam Mim, a dreadful old witch.

"Oh, please, I'm not really a sparrow," chirped Wart. "I'm a boy. The great Merlin changed me with his wonderful magic."

At this the witch hissed with anger. "Wonderful magic, bah!" she jeered. "He's just a bungler! Obviously you've never heard of me—the marvelous Madam Mim!"

Watching fearfully from the window, Archimedes thought, *If I don't bring Merlin here in time, Mim will surely do something terrible to that boy.*

When Merlin appeared, Madam Mim refused to hand Wart over. Instead, she challenged Merlin to a Wizards' Duel.

She started the duel by turning into a crocodile. Immediately Merlin turned into a tiny turtle and hid inside his hat; and when the crocodile found him there, he turned into a rabbit and nimbly hopped away. Turning into a fox, the witch ran after him.

But then the rabbit turned into a hunting dog. Madam Mim turned from fox to tiger, only to find that the dog had turned into a sharp-clawed crab. Furious at having her nose pinched, she turned into a sharp-horned rhino. As a mouse, Merlin easily eluded the lumbering rhino. But then, calling on her blackest magic, Madam Mim turned into a fearsome, flame-spewing dragon.

Wart gulped with dismay. What could poor Merlin turn into now?

He turned into a rare disease called Purple Pox which was very catching. In an instant the dragon broke out all over in a rash of great purple spots. Anyone sick with Purple

Pox had to stay in bed for two whole weeks. And so Merlin clearly was the winner of the duel.

Time passed.

Winter came and Kay was knighted. He was all ready for the tournament to be held on New Year's Day when suddenly his squire fell ill. So Sir Ector let Wart be Kay's squire after all. And they all set forth proudly to London Town.

The tournament field at London Town was full to the brim on New Year's Day. A great crowd sat in the grandstand. As they watched the tilting, they wondered which brave knight would win and so become their king.

Sir Ector clapped Kay on the shoulder. "You'll win, boy!" he cried. "Dash it all, I feel it in my bones!"

Just then there came a dismal moan from Wart. In his excitement he had forgotten Kay's sword. It was back at the inn where they had slept.

Kay was furious when he heard this. "You bungling little fool!" he cried.

"Oh, please, Kay," said Wart. "I'll fetch it for you."

"You'd better fetch it!" Kay shouted after him as he ran off. "Or don't you dare come back!"

Wart ran his fastest, but when he got to the inn it was closed. Everyone had gone to the tournament.

A sword! He had to have a sword!

Wart ran frantically along the street until he came to a quiet churchyard. And there was a heavy stone with an anvil on it, and a gleaming sword was stuck through the anvil.

With a sigh of relief Wart ran up to the sword, drew it out gently, and carried it back to the tournament field.

"But *that's* not Kay's sword," said Sir Ector when he saw it.

Noticing some letters written in gold below the hilt, Sir Ector took the sword from Wart's hands. He held it closely and read:

WHOSO PULLETH OUT THIS SWORD OF THIS STONE AND ANVIL IS RIGHT-WISE KING BORN OF ENGLAND.

The nobleman turned white, for suddenly he remembered the old story of the Sword in the Stone.

"Wart," he said hoarsely, "where did you get this?"

"Outside a church," said Wart. "It was stuck in an anvil."

By now a crowd of noblemen had gathered around. They all looked at the sword and they looked at Wart.

"Wart," said Sir Ector, his voice still hoarse, "we will all go back to the church at once."

At the church Wart replaced the sword in the stone, then gently drew it out again. But when Kay pulled at it with all his strength, he could not stir the sword. A sigh of wonder rose from the crowd.

Sir Ector, who was a very loyal Englishman, kneeled down before Wart. He forced Kay to kneel down, too.

"Please don't," said Wart. "Let me help you up, sir."

Someone asked, "What's the lad's name?"

"Wart," said Kay.

"Nonsense," snapped Archimedes. "His real name is Arthur."

At this there was a clap of thunder and Merlin made one of his magical appearances. "King Arthur!" he said. "So that's who dropped in to tea!"

"Hail King Arthur!" roared the crowd. "Long live King Arthur!"

As it happens, King Arthur lived very long. What is more important—he was a great and very noble king.

CINDERELLA

ONCE UPON A TIME in a far-off land, there lived a kindly gentleman. He had a fine home and a lovely little daughter, and he gave her all that money could buy—a horse of her own, a funny puppy dog, and many beautiful dresses to wear.

But the little girl had no mother. She did wish for a mother and for other children to play with. So her father married a woman with two daughters. Now, with a new mother and sisters, he thought, his little daughter had everything to make her happy.

69

But alas! the kindly gentleman soon died. His fine home fell into disrepair. And his second wife was harsh and cold. She cared only for her own two ugly daughters. To her lovely stepdaughter she was cruel as cruel could be.

Everyone called the stepdaughter "Cinderella" now. For she had to work hard, she was dressed in rags, and she sat by the cinders to keep herself warm. Her horse grew old, locked up in the barn. And her dog was not allowed in the house.

But do you suppose Cinderella was sad? Not a bit! Cinderella made friends with the birds who flew to her window sill each day. Cinderella made friends with the barnyard chickens and geese. And her best friends of all were—guess who—the mice!

The musty old house was full of mice. Their homes were in the garret, where Cinderella lived. She made little clothes for them, and gave them all names. And they thought Cinderella was the sweetest and most beautiful girl in the world.

Every morning her friends the mice and birds woke Cinderella from her dreams. Then it was breakfast time for the household —with Cinderella doing all the work, of course. Out on the back steps she set a bowl of milk for the stepmother's disagreeable cat, who watched for his chance to catch the mice. The faithful dog had a tasty bone. There was grain for the chickens and ducks and geese. And Cinderella gave some grain to the mice—when they were out of reach of the cat. Then back into the house she went.

Up the stairway she carried breakfast trays for her stepmother and her two lazy stepsisters. And down she came with a basket of mending, some clothes to wash, and a long list of jobs to do for the day.

"Now let me see," her stepmother would say. "You can clean the large carpet in the main hall. And wash all the windows, upstairs and down. Scrub the terrace. Sweep the stairs—and then you may rest."

"Oh," said Cinderella. "Yes. I will finish all those jobs." And off to work she went.

Now across the town from Cinderella's home was the palace of the King. And in the King's study one day sat the King himself.

"The Prince must marry!" said the King to the Great Grand Duke. "It is high time!"

"But, Your Majesty, what can we do?" asked the duke. "First he must fall in love."

"We can arrange that," said the King. "We shall give a great ball, this very night, and invite every girl in the land!"

There was great excitement all through the land. And in Cinderella's home, the stepsisters were delighted, when the invitations to the King's ball arrived.

"How delightful!" they said to each other. "We are going to a ball at the palace!"

"And I—" said Cinderella, "I am invited to the ball, too!"

"Oh, you!" laughed the stepsisters.

"Yes, you!" mocked the stepmother. "Of course you may go, if you finish your work," she said. "And if you have something suitable to wear. I said IF, Cinderella." And she smiled a very horrid smile.

Cinderella worked as hard as she could, all through the long day. But when it was time to leave for the ball, Cinderella had not had a moment to fix herself up, or to give a thought to a dress to wear to the ball.

"Why, Cinderella, you are not ready. How can you go to the ball?" asked her stepmother, when the coach was at the door.

"No. I am not going," said Cinderella sadly.

"Not going! Oh, what a shame!" the stepmother said with her mocking smile. "But there will be other balls."

Poor Cinderella! She went to her room and sank sadly down, with her head in her hands.

But a twittering sound soon made her turn around. Her little friends had not forgotten her. They had been scampering and flying about, as busy as could be, fixing a party dress for her to wear.

"Oh, what a lovely dress!" she cried. "I can't thank. you enough," she told all the birds and the mice. She looked out the window. The coach was still there. So she started to dress for the ball.

"Wait!" cried Cinderella to the coachman. "I am coming too!"

She ran down the long stairway just as the stepmother was giving her daughters some last commands. They turned and stared.

"My beads!" cried one stepsister.

"And my ribbon!" cried the other.

"And those bows! You thief! Those are mine!" shrieked the stepmother.

So they pulled and they ripped and they tore at the dress, until Cinderella was in rags once more. And off they flounced.

Poor Cinderella! She ran to the garden behind the house. And there Cinderella sank down on a low stone bench and wept as if her heart would break.

But soon she felt someone beside her. She looked up, and through her tears she saw a sweet-faced woman. "Oh," said Cinderella. "Good evening. Who are you?"

"I am your fairy godmother," said the little woman. And from the thin air she pulled a magic wand. "Now dry your tears. You can't go to the ball looking like that!

"Let's see now, the first thing you will need is — a pumpkin!" said the fairy godmother.

Cinderella did not understand, but she brought the pumpkin.

"And now for the magic words!" The fairy godmother began, "Salaga doola, menchika boola—bibbidi, bobbidi—boo!"

Slowly, up reared the pumpkin on its pumpkin vine, and it turned into a very handsome magic coach.

"What we need next is some fine big— mice!" said the fairy godmother.

Cinderella brought her friends the mice. And at the touch of the wand they turned into prancing horses.

Then Cinderella's old horse became a very fine coachman.

And Bruno the dog turned into a footman at the touch of the magic wand and a "Bibbidi, bobbidi, boo!"

"There," said the fairy godmother, "now hop in, child. You've no time to waste. The magic only lasts till midnight!"

"But my dress, fairy godmother," said Cinderella as she looked at her rags.

"Good heavens, child!" laughed the fairy godmother. "Of course you can't go in that!"

The wand waved again, and there stood Cinderella in the most beautiful gown in the world, with tiny slippers of glass.

81

The Prince's ball had started. The palace was blazing with lights. The ballroom gleamed with silks and jewels. And the Prince smiled and bowed, but still looked bored, as all the young ladies of the kingdom in turn curtsied before him.

Up above on a balcony stood the King and the Duke looking on. "Whatever is the matter with the Prince?" cried the King. "He doesn't seem to care for one of those beautiful maidens."

"I feared as much," the Great Grand

Duke said. "He will not fall in love easily."

But just then he did! For at that moment Cinderella appeared at the doorway of the ballroom. The Prince caught sight of her through the crowd. And like one in a dream he walked to her side and offered his arm.

Quickly the King beckoned to the musicians, and they struck up a dreamy waltz. The Prince and Cinderella swirled off in the dance. And the King, chuckling over the success of his plan to find a bride for the Prince, went happily off to bed.

All evening the Prince was at Cinderella's side. They danced every single dance. They ate supper together. And Cinderella had such a wonderful time that she quite forgot the fairy godmother's warning until the clock in the palace tower began to strike midnight.

"Oh, dear!" cried Cinderella. She knew the magic was about to end!

Without a word she ran from the ballroom, down the long palace hall, and out the door. One of her little glass slippers flew off, but she could not stop.

She leaped into her coach, and away they raced for home. But as they rounded the first corner the clock finished its strokes. The spell was broken. And there in the street stood an old horse, a dog, and a ragged girl, staring at a small, ordinary pumpkin.

"Glass slipper!" the mice cried.

And Cinderella looked down. Sure enough, there was a glass slipper on the pavement.

"Oh, thank you, godmother!" she said.

Next morning there was great excitement in the palace. The King was furious when he found that the Great Grand Duke had let the beautiful girl slip away.

"All we could find was this one glass slip-per," the Duke admitted. "And now the Prince says he must marry the girl whom this slipper fits. And no one else."

"He did?" cried the King. "He said he would marry her? Well then, find her!"

All day and all night the Grand Duke with his servant traveled about the kingdom, trying to find a foot on which the glass slipper would fit. In the morning, his coach drove up before Cinderella's house.

The news of the search had spread. The stepmother was busy rousing her daughters and preparing them to greet the Duke. She was determined that one of them should wear the slipper and be the Prince's bride.

"The Prince's bride!" whispered Cinderella. "I must dress, too."

She went off to her room, humming a waltzing tune. Then the stepmother suspected the truth—that Cinderella was the girl the Prince was seeking. So the stepmother followed Cinderella—to lock her in her room.

The mice chattered a warning, but Cinderella did not hear them—she was off in a world of dreams.

Then she heard the key click. The door of her room was locked.

"Please let me out—oh, please!" she cried. But the wicked stepmother only laughed and laughed and went away.

"We will save you!" said the loyal mice. "We will somehow get that key!"

The household was in a flurry. The Great Grand Duke had arrived. His servant held the glass slipper in his hand.

"It is mine!" both stepsisters cried.

And each tried to force her foot into the tiny glass slipper. But the stepsisters failed.

Meanwhile, the mice had made themselves into a long, live chain. The mouse at the end dropped down into the stepmother's dress pocket. He popped up again with the key to Cinderella's room! At once the mice hurried off with the key.

Now the Grand Duke was at the door, about to leave. Suddenly, down the stairs Cinderella came flying.

"Oh, wait, wait, please!" she called. "May I try the slipper on?"

"Of course you may try," said the Great Grand Duke. And he called back the servant with the slipper. But the wicked stepmother tripped the boy. Away sailed the slipper, and crash! it splintered into a thousand pieces. "Oh my, oh my!" said the Duke.

"Never mind," said Cinderella. "I have the other here." And she pulled from her pocket the other glass slipper!

So off to the palace went Cinderella in the King's own coach, with the happy Grand Duke by her side. The Prince was delighted to see her again. And so was his father, the King. For this sweet and beautiful girl won the hearts of all who met her.

In no time at all she was Princess of the land. And she and her husband, the charming Prince, rode to their palace in a golden coach to live

Happily Ever After!

LADY AND THE TRAMP

It was on Christmas Eve that Lady came to live with her People, Jim Dear and Darling. They loved her at once, but as often happens they needed some training from her.

For example, they thought she would like a little bed and blankets of her own. It took some howls and whining on Lady's part to show them their mistake. But it was not long before they understood that her place was at the foot of Jim Dear's bed—or Darling's in her turn. People are really quite intelligent, as every dog knows. It just takes a little patience to make them understand.

By the time spring rolled around, Lady had everything under control. Every morning she wakened Jim Dear with a bark and a lick at his hand. She brought his slippers and stood by until he got up.

Then out she raced, through her own small swinging door, to meet the postman at the gate. After the postman came the paper boy; and then it was breakfast time. Lady sat beside Jim Dear and Darling to make certain that not a bite or a crumb go to waste.

After making certain that Darling did not need her help with the housework, Lady went out to circle the house to keep all danger away. She barked at sparrows and dragonflies in a brave and fearless way.

Then she was free to visit around. Lady had two close friends of her own, who lived in the houses on either side of hers. One was an old Scotsman, known to his friends as Jock. The other was a fine old Southern gentleman, Trusty by name. Trusty was a blood-

hound, and in the old days he'd had one of the keenest noses south of the Mason-Dixon Line. Lady, Jock, and Trusty spent many happy days playing together.

Perhaps the nicest part of the day came toward the evening. That was when Jim Dear came home from work. Lady would fly to meet him at his whistle, and scamper home at his side. It took only a moment to reach the little house, and then the family was together again, just the three of them—Jim Dear, Darling, and Lady.

And all this added up to making her the happiest dog in the world.

It was autumn of that year when a bit of urgent business brought a stranger to the neighborhood. The stranger was a cocky young mongrel known around the town simply as "The Tramp." This day he was two jumps ahead of the dog catcher's net, rounding the corner near Lady's house. Just then along the street came a stately open carriage, followed by two proud carriage hounds. The Tramp fell in step with the two proud carriage hounds until the dog catcher gave up the chase and ambled away.

"Understand the pickings are pretty slim around here, eh?" said the Tramp. "A lid on every trash can, a fence around every tree," he had just said, when he saw, from the corner of one twinkling eye, the dog catcher wandering away. "Oh oh!" he barked, and dropped out of step—no marching to someone else's tune for this cocky mongrel!

"Well," the Tramp thought, with a merry cock of his head, "I may as well have a look around this neighborhood as long as I'm here and my time's my own."

And his feet led him down the shady street to the house where Lady lived.

Poor Lady was in a very sad state when the Tramp appeared. The first dark shadow had fallen over her life.

"Why, Miss Lady," Trusty asked her, "is something wrong?"

"Well, Jim Dear wouldn't play when I went to meet him—and then he called me That Dog!" Lady admitted sadly.

"Jim Dear called you, 'That Dog!' " cried Jock. He and Trusty were shocked. But they tried to make light of it.

"I wouldn't worry my wee head about it," Jock told her as cheerily as he could. "Remember, they're only humans after all."

"Yes, I try," said Lady, with tears in her dark eyes. "But Darling and I have always enjoyed our afternoon romps together. But yesterday she wouldn't go out for a walk at all, and when I picked up a soft ball she dropped, and got ready for a game, she said, 'Drop that, Lady!' And she struck me—yes, she struck me."

To Lady's surprise, Jock and Trusty were laughing now.

"Don't take it too seriously," Jock explained. "Don't you see, Lassie, Darling's expecting a wee bairn?"

"Bairn?" said Lady.

"He means a baby, Miss Lady," Trusty said.

"What's a baby or a bairn, Jock?" Lady wanted to know. Just as Jock began to answer

Lady's question, the Tramp came trotting along.

"Well," said Jock, staring thoughtfully, "they resemble humans, only they're smaller. They walk on all fours—"

"And if I remember correctly," Trusty broke in, "they holler a lot."

"They're very expensive," Jock warned her. "You'd not be permitted to play with them."

"But they're mighty sweet," smiled Trusty.

"And very, very soft," said Jock.

"Just a cute little bundle of trouble," a new voice broke in. It was the Tramp, who swaggered up to join the group. "They scratch, pinch, pull ears," he went on to say, "but any dog can take that. It's what they do to your happy home! Homewreckers, that's what they are! Just you wait, Miss, you'll see what happens when Junior's here.

"You get the urge for a nice comfortable scratch, and—'Put that dog out,' they say. 'He'll get fleas on the baby.'"

"You start barking at a strange mutt, and —'Stop that racket,' they say. 'You'll wake up the baby.'"

"No more of those nice juicy cuts of beef. Left over baby food for you!

"Instead of your nice warm bed by the fire—a leaky dog house in the rain!"

"Oh dear!" sobbed Lady.

Jock rushed to her side. "Don't you listen, Lassie," he growled. "No human is that cruel."

"Of course not, Miss Lady," Trusty put in. "Don't believe it. Everyone knows, a dog's best friend is his human!"

"Ha ha," laughed the Tramp, as he turned to leave. "Just remember this, pigeon. A human's heart has only just so much room for love and affection, and when a baby moves in—the dog moves out!"

Poor Lady! She had a long time to worry—all through the long dreary winter months. At last, on a night of wind and rain, in a most confusing flurry, the baby came.

Now there was a stranger in Lady's old room. Lady was scarcely allowed inside the door. And when she did follow Darling in, all she could see was a small high bed, and a strange wrapped-up shape in Darling's arms. But there was a smile on Darling's lips, and a softness in Darling's eyes. When she spoke she spoke softly, and often sang sweet songs. So Lady began to think the baby must indeed be something sweet—if only they could be friends and play! Perhaps it might have worked out that way soon, if only Jim Dear had not been called away!

"I'll only be gone a few days," Jim Dear explained to Lady, with an old-time pat on the head. "Aunt Sarah will be here to help you, and I'm counting on you to—"

Knock! Knock!

The door shook under a torrent of bangs. It was Aunt Sarah. Lady watched from between Jim Dear's legs as a stern-faced lady marched in, leaving a stack of luggage on the door step for Jim Dear to bring in.

"I'll put your bags away for you, Aunt Sarah," Jim Dear offered.

"No need for that, James. You just skedaddle or you'll miss your train."

"Oh—er, all right, Aunt Sarah," Jim Dear said. As he rushed toward the door, he managed a last pat for Lady. "It's going to be a little rough for a while," she understood from his pat. "But it won't be long, and remember, Lady, I'm depending on you to watch over things while I'm away."

Then Jim Dear was gone, quite gone.

Lady knew her job. She raced upstairs, to the bed where Darling was having her afternoon rest. And Lady snuggled down on the coverlet, within patting distance of her hand.

Not for long though!

"What is that animal doing here?" Lady heard Aunt Sarah's voice.

"Oh, it's just Lady," Darling smiled.

"Get off that bed," snapped Aunt Sarah— and she pushed Lady. "You'll get fleas on the baby! Shoo! Shoo!"

Poor Lady! She was hustled straight out of the room, back down to the front hall. There, still waiting, stood Aunt Sarah's bags, so she gave them an experimental sniff.

There was something peculiar about one basket—an odor unfamiliar to Lady and one she did not understand. She sniffed again. She circled the basket. Zip! Out shot a silken paw and clawed her from behind!

Lady pounced on the basket. Suddenly out shot two large forms! Yes, two Siamese cats. They were very sly, they were very sleek, they were tricky as could be.

They walked across the mantelpiece, scratched the best table legs, they bounced on the pillows Lady never touched—but whenever Aunt Sarah came into the room, they made it seem that Lady had done everything bad, and they had been angel twins!

"Get away, little beast!" Aunt Sarah would say, kicking at Lady with a toe. "Poor darlings," she would coo, scooping up the Siamese cats in her arms. "Dogs don't belong in the house with you!"

Poor Lady! She was blamed for trying to catch the goldfish, when really she was just protecting them from the cats. And when the cats opened the canary cage and were chasing the poor frightened little thing—it was Lady who was blamed by Aunt Sarah, of course, and put out at night in the rain! Everything was just as the Tramp had said. Oh, what a sad, sad life!

The worst day of all was still to come. That was the day Aunt Sarah took Lady to the pet shop and bought her a muzzle!

"It isn't safe to have this beast around in the house with a baby unmuzzled," she said. Tears filled poor Lady's eyes. Then the muzzle was snapped on. "There now, you little brute!" said Aunt Sarah.

Lady could stand no more. She reared back on her strong little legs until her leash snapped through. And away our Lady ran.

She had never been alone in the city. The large crowds of people frightened her, and the clatter of hurrying wheels. Down a dim and quiet alley she ran, and she found a hiding place behind a big barrel. There she lay and shook with fright.

"Well, pigeon, what are you doing here?" she heard a brisk voice say.

It was the Tramp, and how handsome he looked to Lady, how big and strong! She

snuggled her head on his manly chest and had herself a good cry.

"There there," he said in a gentler tone. "Get it out of your system and then tell me what this is all about."

So Lady told him the whole sad story.

"And I don't know what to do next," she told him with a sob.

"First of all we've got to get rid of that catcher's mitt," said the Tramp, with a nod at her muzzle. "Let's see—a knife? No, that's for humans. A scissors? A saw? Teeth! That's what we need. Come on, we'll visit the zoo."

Lady had never heard of a zoo, but she trustingly followed along. And Lady did just as the Tramp told her to, until they were safely past the No Dogs sign, strolling down the sunny paths inside the zoo.

The paths were lined with high fences,

and beyond the fences—well, never in her wildest dreams had Lady imagined that animals came in such a variety of sizes and shapes and colors. But though all of them were nice about it, there did not seem to be one who could help remove the muzzle—until they came to the Beaver House.

"Say," said the Tramp, "if ever a fellow was built to cut, it's Beaver. Let's call on him." So they did.

"That's a pretty cute gadget," Beaver said, pointing at Lady's muzzle. "Did you make it yourself?"

"Oh no," said Lady.

"We were hoping you could help us get it off," the Tramp explained.

"Get that muzzle off? Hm, let's have a look at it. No, I'm afraid not. The only way I can get it off is to chew through it, and that seems a shame . . ."

"That's exactly what we had in mind," grinned the Tramp.

"It is?" The Beaver was surprised. "Well, it's your thingamajig. Hold still now. This may hurt a bit."

Lady held as still as could be.

"There!" said Beaver. And with a smile he handed her the muzzle. She was free.

"It's off! It's off!" cried Lady, bouncing up and down the paths with joy. "Oh, thank you, thank you," she stopped to say, as the Tramp prepared to lead her off.

"Here!" said the Beaver. "You're forgetting something—your gadget."

"Keep it if you wish, Beaver," said the Tramp with a lordly air.

"I can?" marveled Beaver. "Well, say, thanks." And as they looked back he was trying it on with a happy smile.

"The question is, what do you want to do now, pigeon?" the Tramp asked.

"Oh, I'll have to go home now," Lady said.

"Home?" said the Tramp. "You go home now and you'll just be sliding your head into another muzzle. Stay away a few hours, let them worry. Give Aunt Sarah a chance to cool off. Have dinner with me at a little place I know, and then I'll show you the town."

Lady had never known anyone so masterful. She found herself following along. And she had to admit that dinner on the back step of a little restaurant was the best meal she'd had for weeks. Then they went to the circus—Lady's first; they had wonderful seats under the first row.

After the circus, Lady and Tramp took a stroll in the park, and since it was spring and the night was warm, and they were young, time passed all too quickly. The first rays of morning caught Lady by surprise.

"Oh dear," she said. "I must go home."

"Look," said Tramp, "they've given you a pretty rough time. You don't owe them a thing. Look at the big wide world down here. It's ours for the taking, pigeon."

"It sounds wonderful," Lady admitted, "but it leaves out just one thing—a baby I promised to watch over and protect."

The Tramp gave a deep sigh.

"You win," he said. "I'll take you home."

But on the way they passed a chicken yard. Tramp could not resist.

"Ever chase chickens Lady? No? Then you've never lived." In a flash, he was scraping a hole under the fence.

"But we shouldn't," said Lady.

"That's why it's fun," the Tramp explained.

So she followed him in; and when the chickens squawked and the farmer came running, it was Lady who was caught. Oh, the Tramp tried to warn her, but she simply didn't know her way around. The next thing she knew, she was in the Dog Pound!

Lady had never met dogs like those she found in the Pound. At first they frightened her. But she soon found they had hearts of gold—and she found they knew the Tramp.

"Now there's a bloke what never gets caught!" said one.

FRESH EGGS

"Yup, his only weakness is dames,' said another. "Got a new one every week."

"He does?" said Lady. "Well, I certainly hope I wouldn't give a second thought to a person like that!" But really she felt very sad. She was sure now the Tramp had let her be caught so he could go on to another "dame."

Her reception when she got home did not make her feel any better. She was put out in the dog house on a stout chain!

When the Tramp came around to call, early the next day, Lady would not even speak to him. That was just what one stranger in the yard had hoped to see. The stranger was slinking silently along under the dark cover of the tall grass near the fence. From the end of the fence it was a short dash to the shelter of the woodpile. And there the stranger lurked, waiting for the darkness— that arch-enemy of all society, the rat!

The rat was no stranger in one way. He had often poked around this house, trying to find a way in. But always he had been frightened off by the thought of a dog on guard.

Now, seeing Lady safely chained far from the back door, and having watched her send the Tramp away, the rat thought his big chance had come at last!

So in the dim light of dusk, he left his hiding place and scurried toward the back door.

Lady was standing at her dog house doorway, looking sadly after the Tramp, and wondering if she had been too cruel, not to let him try to explain—when she saw it—that sly, evil figure slinking toward her house—toward Darling and the baby!

Lady had never seen a rat before, but some instinct told her that this creature was evil and vicious. She knew this stranger must not be allowed in the house!

When she saw it slinking through her own little swinging door, Lady went wild with rage! Barking wildly, she lunged against the chain. Far down the street, the Tramp heard her and stopped in his tracks.

Upstairs in the house, Aunt Sarah heard too, but she was not one to understand.

"Lady! Stop that racket!" she snapped, then slammed the window and turned away.

Darling heard the uproar. "What is it, Aunt Sarah?" she asked.

"Nothing, Elizabeth, but that spoiled brat carrying on because she's chained up."

"But she's never carried on like this before," Darling worried. "Could someone be

trying to break into the house? Perhaps if we went down to see?"

"Nonsense," snapped Aunt Sarah. "Stop being ridiculous and go back to sleep, Elizabeth. And you—hush up, you little beast!"

At that very moment the evil rat was pulling himself step by step up the stairs.

But at that moment, too, the Tramp came back. He wondered why Lady was barking.

"What's wrong, pigeon?" he asked.

"A horrible creature—went in the house," Lady panted anxiously.

"Horrible creature? Sure you're not seeing things, pigeon?"

"Oh, please, please!" cried Lady. "Don't you understand? Tramp, please! The baby—we must protect the baby!"

With one last lunge she snapped the chain; staggering forward, she broke into a run, and raced fearlessly for the back door.

The Tramp was close behind her. "Take it easy," he told her in his firm soothing tones, "remember I'm right with you."

Through the kitchen they raced, side by side in the darkness; then into the hall and up the stairs. Lady led the way to the baby's room and the Tramp followed close behind. But just inside the door they both stopped short, for there sure enough was the rat!

The Tramp knew what to do, and he wasted no time. He disposed of the rat behind a chair in the corner, while Lady stood guard over the crib.

The Tramp was just returning, still panting from his battle with the rat, when Aunt Sarah, broom in hand, appeared. "Take that, you mangy cur!" she cried, lowering the broom on the Tramp.

He winced and ran before the weapon— and found himself locked in a dark closet!

Now Darling was there too, cuddling the baby, as she sang sweet songs.

"Lady," Darling said in surprise, "whatever got into you?"

"Humph!" said Aunt Sarah. "She's jealous of the baby and brought one of her vicious friends in to attack the child."

"Oh, I'm sure not," cried Darling. "I believe that she saw the stray and came in to protect the baby."

"Rubbish!" said Aunt Sarah. "But Lady is your responsibility. If you don't know your duty, I know mine. I will notify the authorities. They'll take care of this other brute once and for all. As for you—" she picked Lady up by the scruff of her neck—"I'm locking you in the kitchen for the night."

Bad news travels fast in the animal world. By morning everybody in the neighborhood knew—every pigeon, canary and squirrel— that the Tramp had been picked up and was to be taken off to be executed. Aunt Sarah's cats knew, and for once even they felt something like sympathy as they tiptoed past the kitchen where Lady sobbed alone.

Jock and Trusty heard it; they watched from behind the shrubbery as the Dog Pound Wagon stopped at the door, and the catcher came out, leading the Tramp to his doom.

"We misjudged him badly," Jock admitted.

"Yes," said Trusty. "He's a very brave lad. And Miss Lady's taking it very hard."

"There must be some way we can help," said Jock to Trusty. But they could not think what it would be.

Lady knew, though, there was just one chance. And it came when a taxi stopped at the door. Jim Dear was home at last!

Darling told Jim Dear the story of their terrible night as soon as he came in.

"But I still don't understand," said Jim. "Why should a strange dog—and Lady—?"

Lady, leaping at the kitchen door, tried to say that she could explain.

Jim Dear opened the door and knelt beside her while she jumped up to lick his face.

"Lady, what's all this about, old girl? You know the answer, I'm sure," he said.

For a reply, Lady jumped past Jim Dear and raced up the stairs to the baby's room.

"She's trying to tell us something," he said.

Jim Dear was at Lady's heels.

"You're right, dear," she said. And when Lady showed her the dead rat behind the chair, at last she knew what it was.

"Don't you see?" he cried. "That strange dog wasn't attacking the baby. He was helping Lady protect it instead."

"Oh, Jim Dear, and we've sent him off—" Darling wailed, clasping her hands.

"I don't see the reason for all this fuss," Aunt Sarah sternly said.

"Aunt Sarah," said Jim, "I'm going to save that dog. And you are going to leave."

"Well, I never!" Aunt Sarah gasped.

Then off raced Jim Dear in the taxicab, on the trail of the Dog Pound cart. But Lady was ahead of him. With Trusty and Jock beside her, Lady was off, down through the street and through the town on the wagon's trail.

They made some wrong turns. There were some dead ends. But at last they sighted the cart ahead, with the Tramp watching them through the wire mesh.

Straight to the horse's feet the three dogs ran. Then barking and snapping and leaping about, Trusty, Jock, and Lady set the horse to rearing nervously until the whole cart swayed and tipped! They had won!

Now up rattled Jim Dear's taxicab.

"That dog," cried Jim Dear, pointing to the Tramp, rubbing noses with Lady through the bars. "It's all been a terrible mistake."

"You mean that mongrel is yours, Mister?" the driver asked.

"Yes," said Jim Dear. "He's mine."

So home Lady and the Tramp went, in a taxicab with Jim Dear. And that was the end of the story—almost.

Let us visit that little house once more, at merry Christmas time. See the Baby playing on the floor, surrounded by wiggling puppy dogs. Jim Dear and Darling are watching Baby, with love and pride in their eyes. And watching the puppies are Lady and the Tramp.

SNOW WHITE
AND THE SEVEN DWARFS

Once upon a time in a far-away land, a lovely Queen sat by her window sewing. As she worked, she pricked her finger with her needle. Three drops of blood fell on the snow-white linen.

"How happy I would be if I had a little girl with lips as red as blood, skin as white as snow, and hair as black as ebony!" thought the Queen as she sewed.

When spring came, her wish was granted. But the Queen's happiness was very brief. As she held her lovely baby in her arms, the Queen whispered, "Little Snow White!" and then she died.

When the lonely King married again, his new Queen was beautiful. But, alas, she was also very heartless and cruel. She was very jealous of all the lovely ladies of the kingdom, but most jealous of all of the lovely little Princess, Snow White.

Now the Queen's most prized possession was her magic mirror. Every day she looked into it and asked:

> *"Mirror, mirror on the wall,*
> *Who is the fairest of us all?"*

If the magic mirror replied that she was the fairest in the kingdom, all was well. But if another lady was named, the Queen flew into a furious rage. She would summon her huntsman and have her killed.

As the years passed, Snow White grew more and more beautiful, and her sweet nature made everyone in the kingdom love her —everyone but the Queen.

The Queen's chief fear was that Snow White might grow to be the fairest in the land. So she banished the young Princess to the servants' quarters. She made Snow White dress in rags, and forced her to slave from morning to night.

But while she worked and lived in the servants' quarters, Snow White dreamed dreams of a handsome Prince who would come some day and carry her off to his castle in the clouds. And as she dusted and scrubbed—and dreamed—Snow White grew more beautiful day by day.

At last came the day the Queen had been dreading. She asked:

"Mirror, mirror on the wall,
Who is the fairest of us all?"

and the mirror replied:

"Her lips blood red, her hair like night,
Her skin like snow, her name—
Snow White!"

The Queen's face grew pale with anger. The Queen rushed from the room and called her huntsman to her.

"Take Princess Snow White into the forest and bring me back her heart in this jeweled box," she said.

112

The huntsman bowed his head in grief. He had no choice but to obey the cruel Queen's commands.

Snow White had no fear of the kindly huntsman. She went happily into the forest with him. It was beautiful there among the trees, and the Princess, not knowing what was in store for her, skipped along beside the huntsman, now stopping to pick violets, now singing a happy tune.

The huntsman watched Snow White as she skipped and sang through the forest. At last the poor huntsman could bear it no longer. He fell to his knees before the Princess.

"I cannot kill you, Princess," he said, "even though it is the Queen's command. Run into the forest and hide, but you must never return to the castle."

Then away went the huntsman. On his way back to the castle, he killed a small animal and took its heart in the jeweled box to the wicked Queen.

Alone in the forest, Snow White wept with fright. Deeper and deeper into the woods she ran, half blinded by tears. It seemed to her that roots of trees reached up to trip her feet, that branches reached out to clutch at her dress as she passed.

At last, weak with terror, Snow White fell to the ground. As the sun began to set, she lay there, sobbing her heart out.

Ever so quietly, out from burrows and nests and hollow trees, crept the little woodland animals. Bunnies and tiny chipmunks,

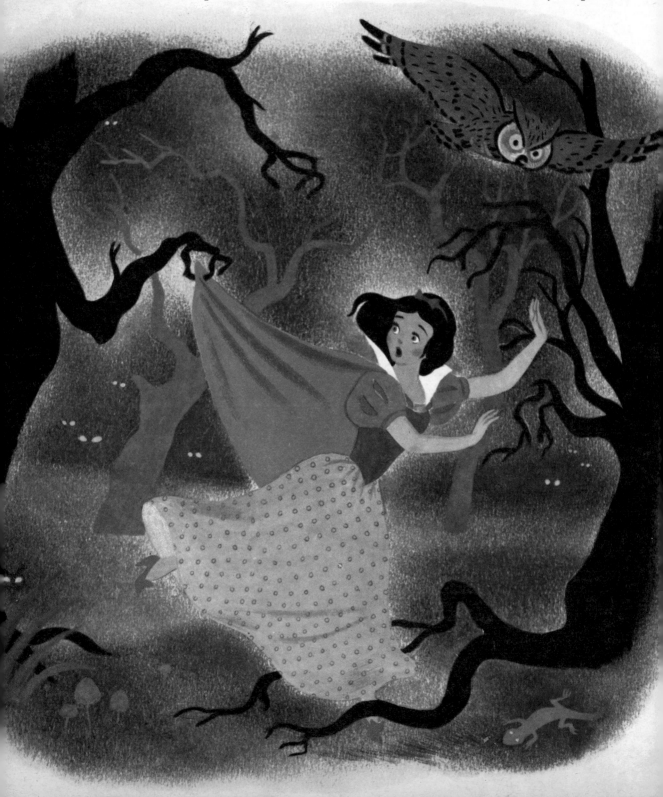

raccoons and squirrels, all gathered around. When Snow White looked up and saw them there, she smiled through her tears. At the sight of her smile, the little animals crept closer, snuggling in her lap or nestling in her arms. The birds sang their gayest melodies to Snow White, and the little forest clearing was filled with joy.

"I feel ever so much better now," Snow White told her new friends. "But I still do need a place to sleep."

One of the birds chirped something, and the little animals nodded in agreement. Then off flew the birds, leading the way. The rabbits,

chipmunks and squirrels followed after, and Snow White came with her arm around the neck of a gentle mother deer.

At last, through a tangle of brush, Snow White saw a tiny cottage which was nestled in a clearing up ahead.

"It's just like a doll's house," she cried.

Skipping across a little bridge to the house, Snow White peeked in through one window pane. There seemed to be no one at home, but the sink was piled high with cups and saucers and plates which looked as though they had never been washed. Dirty little shirts and wrinkled little trousers hung over chairs, and everything was blanketed with dust.

"Maybe the children who live here have no mother," said Snow White, "and need someone to take care of them. Let's clean their house and surprise them."

So in she went, followed by her forest friends. Snow White found an old broom in the corner and swept the floor.

Then Snow White washed all the crumpled little clothes, and set a big kettle of delicious soup to bubbling on the hearth.

"Now," she said to the animals, "let's see what is upstairs."

Up they all went. They found seven little beds all in a row.

"Why, they have their names carved on them," said Snow White. "Doc, Happy, Sneezy, Dopey—such funny names for children! Grumpy, Bashful, Sleepy! My, I'm a little sleepy myself!"

Yawning, Snow White sank down across the little beds and fell asleep. Quietly the little animals stole away, and the birds flew out the window. All was still in the tiny little house in the forest.

"Hi ho, hi ho,
    It's home from work we go—"

Seven little men came marching through the woods, singing on their way. As they came in sight of their cottage, they stopped short. Smoke was curling from the chimney, and the door was standing open!

"Look! Someone's in our house!"

"Maybe it's a ghost—or a goblin—or even a demon!"

"I knew it," said one of the little men with a grumpy look. "I've been warning you for two hundred years something awful was about to happen!"

At last, on timid tiptoe, in they went.

"Someone's stolen our dishes," growled the grumpy one.

"No, they're hidden in the cupboard," said Happy, with a grin. "But hey! My cup's been washed! Sugar's all gone!"

At that moment a sound came from upstairs. It was Snow White yawning.

"It's up there—the goblin—er demon—er ghost!" said one of the scared little men.

Shouldering their pick axes, up the stairs they went—seven frightened little dwarfs.

The seven little men stood in a row at the foot of their beds. They all stared at the sleeping Snow White.

"Wh-what is it?" whispered one. "It's mighty purty," said another. "Why, bless my soul, I think it's a girl!" said a third. And then Snow White woke up.

"Why, you're not children," she exclaimed. "You're little men. Let me see if I can guess your names."

And she did—Doc and Bashful, Happy, Sleepy, and Sneezy, and last of all Dopey and Grumpy, too.

"Supper is not quite ready," said Snow White. "You'll have just enough time to wash and change your clothes."

"Wash!" cried the little men with horror in their tones. They hadn't washed for oh, it seemed hundreds of years. But out they marched, when Snow White insisted. And it was worth it in the end. For such a supper they had never tasted. Nor had they ever had such an evening of fun. All the forest folk gathered around the cottage windows to watch them play and dance and sing.

Back at the castle, the huntsman had presented to the wicked Queen the box which, she thought, held Snow White's heart.

"Ah ha!" she gloated. "At last!" And down the castle corridors she hurried straight to her magic mirror. Then she asked:

"Now, magic mirror on the wall,
Who is the fairest one of all?"

But the honest mirror replied:

"With the seven dwarfs will spend the night
The fairest in the land, Snow White."

Then the Queen realized that the huntsman had tricked her. She flung the jeweled box at the mirror, shattering the glass into a thousand pieces. Then, shaking with rage, the Queen hurried down to a dark cave below the palace where she worked her Black Magic.

First she disguised herself as a toothless old woman dressed in tattered rags. Then she searched her books of magic spells for a horrid spell to work on Snow White.

"What shall it be?" she muttered to herself. "The poisoned apple, the Sleeping Death? Perfect!"

In a great kettle she stirred up a poison brew. Then she dipped an apple into it—one, two, three—and the apple came out a beautiful rosy red, the most tempting apple you could hope to see.

Cackling with wicked pleasure, the Queen dropped her poisoned apple into a basket of fruit and started on her journey to the home of the seven dwarfs.

She felt certain that her plan would succeed, for the magic spell of the Sleeping Death could be broken only by Love's First Kiss. The Queen was certain no lover would find Snow White, asleep in the forest.

It was morning when the Queen reached
the great forest, close to the dwarf's cottage.
From her hiding place she saw Snow White
saying good-bye to the seven little men as
they marched off to work.

"Now be careful!" they warned her.
"Watch out for the Queen."

But when the poor, ragged old woman
with a basket of apples appeared outside her
window, Snow White never thought to be
afraid. She gave the old woman a drink of
water and spoke to her kindly.

Thank you, my dear," the Queen cackled. "Now in return won't you have one of my beautiful apples?" And she held out to Snow White the poisoned fruit.

Down swooped the little birds and animals on the wicked Queen.

"Stop it!" Snow White cried. "Shame on you." The she took the poisoned apple and bit into it, and fell down lifeless on the cottage floor.

Away went the frantic birds and woodland animals into the woods to warn the seven dwarfs. Now the dwarfs had decided not to do their regular jobs that day. They were hard at work, making a gift for Snow White, to tell her of their love.

The seven little dwarfs looked up in surprise as the birds and animals crowded around them. At first they did not understand. Then they realized that Snow White must be in danger. "The Queen!" they cried, and they ran for home.

The little men were too late. They came racing into the clearing just in time to see the Queen slide away into the shadows. They chased her through the gloomy woods until she plunged into a bottomless gulf and disappeared forever.

129

When the dwarfs came home, they found Snow White lying as if asleep. They built her a bed of crystal and gold, and set it up in the forest. There they kept watch, night and day, hoping she might awake.

After a time a handsome Prince of a nearby kingdom heard travelers tell of the lovely Princess asleep in the forest, and he rode there to see her. At once he knew that he loved her truly, so he knelt beside her and kissed her lips.

At the touch of Love's First Kiss, Snow White awoke. There, bending over her, was the Prince of her dreams. Snow White knew that she loved him, too. She said good-bye to the seven dwarfs and, mounted on a white charger behind her Prince, rode off to his Castle of Dreams Come True.

101 DALMATIANS

A DAMP BEGINNING

NOT LONG ago there lived in London a Dalmatian called Pongo. Pongo had a human "pet," Roger Radcliff. Like most humans, Roger thought that people owned their dogs. But like most dogs, Pongo knew better.

The two young bachelors would probably have lived on in their cluttered little flat, if Pongo hadn't happened to look out of the window one fine spring day.

He was looking out of the window because he was tired of looking at the mess inside the flat. Dirty coffee cups were piled high on the mantelpiece. One of Roger's ties was draped over the lampshade. And papers were scattered all over the floor. Roger was a song writer, and as he sat at the piano, humming and playing tunes, he was apt to forget about such unimportant things as waste-paper baskets and ashtrays.

"Something has to be done," thought Pongo, as he gazed out of the window.

Suddenly Pongo sat up very straight. A beautiful Dalmatian, her head carried high, was trotting demurely past the window. With her was an equally beautiful lady.

"That's it!" thought Pongo. "We need mates. Preferably tidy ones, and those two look just right."

It was just four-fifteen by the battered old clock on the mantel. Pongo always took Roger for a walk promptly at five o'clock. It was an easy matter for Pongo to turn the hands of the clock forward with his nose. Then he barked to attract Roger's attention.

"Hmm," said Roger, "is it five already?" He absent-mindedly set his watch hands to match those of the clock, and then he searched for his hat.

"Time for your walk in the park, old boy," said Roger. "Now where is your leash?" But Pongo was already holding it in his mouth, his tail wagging joyfully.

"We must hurry," thought Pongo, "or we'll be too far behind." And as Roger opened the door, the dog leaped forward with a bound, tugging his pet behind him.

Pongo headed for the park, pulling so hard on the leash that Roger almost had to run to keep up with him.

"Pongo, boy," cried Roger. "Take it easy. What's the hurry?"

But the dog hurried on, looking this way and that, darting down side paths and peering into shaded nooks. And suddenly he found them. The girl was seated on a bench reading, and the beautiful Dalmatian was by her side, watching the swans on the lake. It was a perfect situation, Pongo knew, if he could only take advantage of it.

"I can't depend on Roger," thought Pongo. "I know what he'll do. He'll settle down on the grass and puff his pipe, and that will be it. It's up to me."

Pongo led Roger slowly past the bench. Roger was staring straight ahead, but the girl looked up from her book and her dog cast Pongo a shy glance. Then Roger did exactly what Pongo had expected. He sat down on the grass, with his back to the girl, and slowly puffed his pipe.

Quickly Pongo snatched Roger's hat from his head and started to cavort about the bench.

"Pongo, you crazy hound!" shouted Roger. "Come on. Let's have it back, boy."

But Pongo continued his gamboling, and finally dropped his hat on the young lady's bench.

It worked. Roger had finally seen the girl. But as Pongo continued to bark wildly, chase pigeons, and generally show off, the girl gave a sigh of exasperation and closed her book.

"Come, Perdita," she called to her dog. "There's no use trying to read." They rose to leave.

Roger caught Pongo with a flying tackle, and snapped the leash onto his collar.

"Come on, you old renegade," he said. "We're going home. You know, Pongo, you're getting to be quite a rascal. What's come over you?" Roger turned resolutely toward home.

But Pongo wasn't giving up without one more try. In desperation he ran around the girl, then wheeled back in a circle towards Roger, winding the two of them up in his leash.

"Oh! I beg your pardon! So sorry . . . I . . ." stammered Roger, as he and the girl struggled to keep their balance.

"Well, I never in all my life . . ." the girl started to say, but the rest of her words were lost in a loud SPLASH! Roger and the girl had fallen into the lake. The girl's dog looked on in shocked silence, while Pongo, trying to make amends, retrieved the girl's hat. It was a catastrophe.

"Oh," wailed the girl. "My . . . my new spring suit. And . . . and my new hat!"

Roger was flustered and contrite. "Please," he said, "let me help you up. I'm so sorry. My dog has never acted this way before."

"Never mind! Never mind!" said the girl. "Just go away."

She reached into her purse for a handkerchief to dry her face, but the handkerchief was at wet as the rest of her.

"Here," said Roger gallantly, as he reached into his pocket. "Take mine."

Roger made a ridiculous picture as he stood damply in the pond, holding out a dripping kerchief. The girl began to giggle . . . then to laugh. Roger grinned sheepishly. Finally, both of them burst into shrieks of laughter.

Pongo could hardly believe his ears. Somehow his plan had worked.

"There's no figuring out humans," he thought, "or females of any kind for that matter." For the girl's dog was looking at him shyly . . . and he knew he'd been forgiven.

CRUELLA DE VIL

After that, the two dogs and their pets often walked together in the park, and the meeting that had begun in so cold and wet a fashion deepened into warm affection.

The girl's name, Pongo learned, was Anita. Her dog was Perdita, and Pongo thought it the prettiest name he had ever heard.

It wasn't long before Roger and Anita were married, an arrangement that suited Pongo and Perdita admirably.

The four of them moved into a small house near the park. It was a modest little house, but just right for two couples who were starting out. Roger worked at his music on the top floor, in quarters considerably tidier than the old bachelor flat. There was now a round little dumpling of a maid called Nanny, who was a wonderful cook and housekeeper. She was such a kind and understanding soul that Pongo often said he considered her almost canine.

Life in the little flat was pleasant and uneventful for the first few months. And then Cruella De Vil began to pay them visits.

She was a strange woman, an old school friend of Anita's. Roger heartily disliked her, and as for Pongo and Perdita—their instinct was to stay as far away from her as possible.

One day Roger was searching for suitable words to fit his new melody. A screech of brakes drew him to the window, and he groaned, "There she is again—Cruella De Vil."

He turned back to his piano, then suddenly he let out a wild yell.

"Cruella! Cruella De Vil! That's it!"

He started to sing.

"Cruella De Vil . . . Cruella De Vil . . .
If she doesn't scare you, no evil thing will.
She's like a spider waiting for the kill . . .
Cruella . . . Cruella De Vil . . ."

"Shh, Roger. She'll hear you," said Anita, as Cruella swept into the house, trailing her furs behind her.

"Darling, how are you?" gushed Cruella. "And how are your little spotted friends?" She looked thoughtfully at Perdita and Pongo. "They have such *perfectly* beautiful coats." The two dogs backed away nervously. "When do you expect the puppies, and how many of them?"

"Oh, six or seven," answered Anita. "And sometimes as many as nine or ten. But we won't know for another three weeks or so."

Cruella smiled a crafty smile. "Let me know when they arrive, won't you dear?"

she said, and she departed with a swish of her black and white furs.

"Oh Pongo," said Perdita, "what does it mean? Why does she want our puppies? That's all she's after, I know it."

"Don't worry, Perdy," soothed Pongo. "Nothing's going to happen to them. Our pets will see to that."

But Perdita still felt terrified of Cruella.

PUPPIES—AND MORE PUPPIES

The puppies were born one wild and stormy night late in October. Pongo and Roger waited anxiously in the kitchen, while Nanny excitedly announced the arrival of first eight puppies . . . then two more . . . then three additional ones, and finally, fifteen in all.

"Fifteen!" exclaimed Roger. "Pongo, old boy! Can you imagine? FIFTEEN!"

There was a flash of lightning and a roll of thunder, and Cruella De Vil burst unannounced into the room.

"Fifteen puppies!" she cried. "How marvelous! How perfectly, perfectly marvelous!" Before anyone could stop her, she strode over to Perdita's basket and looked down at the puppies.

"Why, they're mongrels! No spots! No spots at all!" cried Cruella in disgust.

"They are *not* mongrels," snapped Nanny Cook. "They'll get their spots. Just wait and see."

"That's right," added Anita. "They'll have their spots in a few weeks."

Cruella smiled an evil smile and reached into her purse for a checkbook.

"Oh, well," she said. "In that case I'll take them all—the whole litter. Just name your price."

"I'm afraid we can't give them up," answered Anita. "Perdita and Pongo would be heartbroken."

"Don't be ridiculous," snapped Cruella. "You can't possibly afford to keep them. You can hardly feed yourselves. What are you going to live on—Roger's songs?" She laughed rudely. "Come now, Anita, when can the puppies leave their mother? In two weeks? Three weeks?"

Roger had been fuming in the background. But now, though he trembled a bit, he stepped forward and stammered:

"We're *not* selling the pup—puppies. N—not a sing—single one—understand? And that's f—final!"

"Why, you horrible man!" screeched Cruella. "*Keep* the little beasts for all I care. But I warn you—I'll get even with you. You *fools*—you *idiots!*" And, stalking out of the house, Cruella slammed the door behind her, so hard that its pane of glass shattered in a hundred pieces.

"Roger," cried Anita joyously, "you were magnificent, darling!"

Nanny Cook clasped her hands in glee. "Oh," she cried, "he was a blooming hero, ma'am! Indeed, he was a blooming hero!"

Quickly, Pongo ran to break the good news to Perdita.

"Perdy," he cried. "We're keeping the puppies—every single one of them. My old pet, Roger, told off that Cruella woman. She's gone! Gone for good!"

"Oh, Pongo," sighed Perdita. "I don't think I've ever been so happy."

THE DOGNAPPERS

They would not have been so happy had they known what Cruella was planning. Over a grimy table in the back room of a tavern, Cruella was talking to two villainous-looking men. One was tall and thin, the other short and fat, but both had shifty eyes and an evil look about them. These were the Baduns, Jasper and Horace.

"Listen carefully to me, you two," said Cruella sternly. "I must have those Dalmatian puppies. Now let me explain my plan to you. . . ."

All was happy, if not exactly quiet, in the little house until one snowy night in December. The puppies had grown, and were now tumbling all over the house. They were more than a handful for Pongo and Perdita. But they loved their pups dearly—all fifteen of them.

That evening, the pups had been particularly rowdy. It was with a sigh of relief that Perdita at last found the smallest pup, Lucky, and tucked him safely into the basket with the others. They were soon all asleep.

"Come on, Perdy," said Pongo. "It's time for our walk."

They brought their leashes to Roger and Anita, and the four of them set out into the park.

In a rickety little truck around the corner, the two Baduns watched.

"There they go for their evening walk," said Jasper.

"Yes," answered Horace, "and nobody home but the little old cook. Let's get on with our business." Stepping up to the front door, Horace pressed the doorbell, and Nanny came to answer the ring.

"We're here to inspect the wiring and the switches," said the Baduns. "We're from the electric company."

"We didn't call for any inspection," said Nanny, and started to close the door.

"It's for your own safety, ma'am," said Horace, and the two ruffians shouldered their way into the house.

"What's the matter with you two?" shouted the furious Nanny. "If you don't get out of this house, I'll call the police."

But while Nanny attached herself firmly to one of the Baduns' coattails and chased him up and down the stairs, the other had accomplished his purpose. In just a matter of moments, the two villains had left through the front door as quickly as they had entered.

"Why, those good-for-nothing hoodlums," sputtered Nanny. "They're nothing but common sneak thieves. I'll bet they've made off with the best silver." She rushed to look. But the silver was undisturbed.

"They were up to something, I'll be bound," she said. "They just wouldn't be— OH . . . THE PUPPIES . . . THE PUPPIES! THEY'RE GONE!"

Panic-stricken, Nanny rushed into the street, but it was too late. The Baduns and their truck and the fifteen puppies had disappeared around the corner.

"Those scoundrels! They took the puppies," cried Nanny. "POLICE! HELP! Oh, can't anybody hear me?"

No one did, and Nanny sank, sobbing, to the curb.

THE TWILIGHT BARK

The papers were full of the news the next morning. "DOGNAPPING. FIFTEEN PUPPIES STOLEN!" said the headlines. There were pictures of the puppies and their parents, and photos of Anita and Roger. Cruella grinned as she saw the pictures.

"Anita and her bashful Beethoven—pipe and all!" She laughed. "Oh, Roger. What a fool you are!"

The ring of the phone interrupted her gleeful perusal of the papers. It was one of the Baduns, and he was frightened.

"We want our money," said Jasper. "The story is in all the papers—with pictures and all. We're getting out of this!"

"Idiot!" shrieked Cruella. "How dare you call me here! You'll get not one penny until

the job's finished. Do you hear?" She slammed down the phone.

But she picked it up again almost immediately.

"Oh, Anita. What a dreadful thing!" she cooed. "I just saw the papers. I couldn't believe it—about the stolen puppies."

"Yes, Cruella," answered Anita. "It was a shock. We're doing everything possible. We even called Scotland Yard, but nothing's been found out yet."

"She's still Number One Suspect in my book," grumbled Roger when Anita had put the phone down. "She's been investigated by Scotland Yard and is supposedly innocent . . . but I don't know . . ."

Pongo looked at them sadly and walked back to Perdita.

"Perdy," he said, "I'm afraid our pets are getting nowhere in their search for our puppies. It looks as if it's up to us."

Perdita was tearful.

"Oh, Pongo!" she wept. "Isn't there any hope?"

"Yes," replied Pongo. *The Twilight Bark.*

"But it's just a gossip chain," began Perdita.

"It's still the fastest way to send news," said Pongo. "And if our puppies are anywhere in the city, the London dogs will know. We'll send the word *tonight*."

It was late and almost dark when Roger and Anita led the two Dalmatians into the park and to the top of Primrose Hill.

Pongo barked the alert--three loud barks and a long howl. At first there was no reply, but finally there came an answer.

"Perdy," said Pongo. "We're in luck. It's the Great Dane over at Hampstead." And Pongo barked out the message.

"Pongo! Quiet, boy!" exclaimed Roger. "Do you want to stir up the whole neighborhood? Come on, old fellow. We're going home."

But the message had been delivered.

Over at Hampstead, the Great Dane was trying to decode the message. A little terrier frisked impatiently about him, bursting with questions: "What is it, Danny? Who's on the telegraph?"

"It's Pongo, Regents Park. It's an all-dog alert," answered Danny.

"What's it all about? What's the word, Danny?" urged the small dog.

"Wait a minute," said Danny, as he translated the barks and yips and howls into the final understandable message. "Well, now! That *is* something. Fifteen puppies stolen—Dalmatians!"

"*Fifteen* puppies?" said the terrier. "Stolen?"

"Yes," replied the Great Dane. "No one knows who did it. Not a clue. Not a trace. They've even called Scotland Yard. The humans have tried everything. Now it's up to us dogs to find them, through the Twilight Bark. I'll send the alert."

The big dog's voice boomed into the night: three loud barks and a long howl. Soon the answering barks started coming in from miles away, every dog wanting to hear the latest news.

Big Danny barked out the message, and from setter to collie, from bulldog to Labrador, the news was relayed.

In a London back alley two old mongrels heard the message as they rummaged through the rubbish cans for food. Said one: "Those puppies aren't in London! They could be anywhere from Plymouth to Newcastle by now."

"Brucey, old lad," said the other, "what do you say we send the word all over England?"

"That's an idea," agreed the first. "I'll leg it for the station at Charing Cross. There are always some dogs going out by freight."

"I'll take the waterfront and tell all the barge dogs," said the other. "Shake a leg, mate." At the River Thames, a small dog on a passing barge barked him a greeting, and in return received Pongo's message as the barge slowly moved by.

The little barge dog wasted no time. As his vessel moved slowly along the moonlit river, he barked the alert at intervals, and to answering greetings he sent out Pongo's message.

The message finally reached the ears of an old hound standing on a hill. "What's going on, Towser?" asked an inquisitive goose, as she joined him on the hilltop. "What's all the gossip?"

"'Tain't gossip, Lucy," he answered. "It's a message all the way from London. Fifteen puppies have been stolen."

"There are no puppies around here," answered the goose. "Except those of Ellen's. And they're all grown up now."

"Then it's up to me to send the word along," answered the old hound. "It'll be up to me to reach the Colonel. He's the only one within barking range."

The goose looked up at the dark night sky. "You'll never reach him at this hour," she warned, waddling off down the hill.

"I can try," said Towser to himself. "I'll bark all night if I have to." He cleared his throat, and once again the alert call went through the night.

HELL HALL

In a stable a few miles away, a retired army horse named Captain was contentedly munching hay. "Hmm," he whinnied, as he heard distant barking. "Sounds like Towser. It's an alert!" He turned to the cat who lay sleeping peacefully on his broad back.

"Sergeant! Sergeant Tibs! Wake up!" he neighed. "A barking signal—an alert. Report to the Colonel at once."

"Yes, sir," said the cat. "Right away, sir." Tibs scampered into the dim shadows of the hayloft in search of his commanding officer.

The Colonel, a gruff old sheepdog, emerged with sleepy eyes and tousled gray hair from a pile of hay.

"Now look here, Tibs," he grumbled, "what's the idea of barging in at this hour of the night?"

"It's an alert, sir," answered Sergeant Tibs. "It's from old Towser down at Withermarsh, sir." The Colonel cocked a long, fuzzy ear toward the barking.

"By Jove," he grunted. "Yes. So it is. I'll see what he wants." His foghorn voice sounded over the hills, and before long there was an answering bark.

"Let's see," said the Colonel. "One long howl . . . two short . . . one yip and a woof. Hmmm . . . I'll have to decode that."

The Colonel listened again. "The next sounds like a number. Four . . . no . . . five woofs. Three fives are thirteen. . . ."

Sergeant Tibs interrupted politely: "That's fifteen, sir." The distant barking continued.

The Colonel was having trouble with his decoding. He lifted his right ear still higher and strained toward the direction of the far-off sounds.

"Hmmm," he murmured. "Dot . . . spot . . . spotted . . . puddings . . . er . . . poodles. Puddles . . . fifteen spotted puddles stolen! Oh, balderdash!" The Colonel glared at the Captain and Sergeant Tibs.

"Try it again, sir," urged Sergeant Tibs. "Ask them to repeat the message."

"Could it be *puppies*, sir?" said Sergeant Tibs, when the distant barking continued. "Fifteen stolen puppies? And that reminds me—two nights ago I heard puppy-barking over at Hell Hall, the old deserted De Vil mansion."

"Nonsense, Tibs!" growled the Colonel. "Nobody's lived there for years!"

The Captain switched his long tail. "Hold on," he said. "Look! There's smoke coming from the chimney."

The Colonel turned to look. "By Jove, so there is! So there is! Humph! I suppose we'll have to investigate!"

With the cat riding on his back, the Colonel plowed through the snow toward the old ruin that once had been a proud mansion.

Tibs, who had heard many tales of the old house being haunted, had to gather up all his courage to climb the tree that stood near the wall. From the wall he leaped onto a narrow ledge, and crept along it till he reached a broken window pane. Carefully, he let himself in.

The house was dark, but suddenly Tibs saw a shaft of light shining under a door. Cautiously he peered into the room beyond.

In a jumble of musty furniture, half-eaten food and odds and ends of their own belongings, lounged two of the most villainous rascals Tibs had even seen.

They were watching a show on a brand-new television set.

But the amazing thing about the room was that, on the floor, on chairs and benches, and curled up on the faded rugs, were *dozens* and *dozens* of *Dalmatian puppies*.

Tibs patiently counted them. He was searching for *fifteen* puppies . . . and here were ninety-nine of them.

"Psst! Youngster!" he whispered to the nearest one. "Are you one of the fifteen stolen puppies?"

"No," the puppy replied. "Most of us came from pet shops in London. But those little ones in front of the television set all have names and collars. Are they the ones you're looking for?"

Tibs was certain that they were. Quickly he retraced his steps to where the Colonel waited and told him the news.

SERGEANT TIBS TO THE RESCUE

The Colonel barked the message to old Towser, who in turn passed it on to a barge dog. From dog to dog the news went on its way toward distant London. Pongo was listening anxiously at the window when he heard Big Danny's voice.

"What is it, Pongo?" asked Perdita.

"It's the Great Dane," answered Pongo. "He has news for us. He'll meet us at Primrose Hill."

"But how will we get out?" said Perdita. She knew it wasn't nearly time for their evening walk.

"Through the back bedroom window," replied Pongo. "It's always open a wee bit. Come on." Pongo raised the window sash with his nose. In an instant the two Dalmatians had jumped from a low roof to the ground, scaled the fence and were on their way to the park. There the Great Dane waited.

"The Pongos! You've made it," he exclaimed with relief. "Good. Your puppies have been found somewhere north of here—in Suffolk."

"Thank heaven!" said Perdita. "Are they all right? Are they safe?"

"That I can't say," replied the big dog. "But I do have a plan to reach them. Can you leave tonight?"

"Yes, of course," said Pongo. "We can leave right away."

The Dane nodded his massive head with satisfaction, and related his plans as the three trotted down the hill.

"I'll go with you as far as Camden Road and give instructions. It's a long trip. Can you read road signs?"

Pongo said that he could, and was rewarded by an admiring look from Perdita.

"When you reach Withermarsh get in touch with old Towser. He'll direct you to the Colonel, and the Colonel will take you to the De Vil place."

"De Vil!" exclaimed Perdita. "Oh, Pongo. It was her!"

"Someone you know?" asked the Great Dane.

"Sorry, sir," answered Pongo, "no time to explain. Oh, I hope we're not too late." And Perdita and Pongo were on their way, running with all their might.

"Good luck, Pongos," barked the Great Dane after them. "If you lose your way, contact the barking chain. They'll be standing by to hear from you."

All night they traveled, pausing only to check their directions with dogs who were awaiting them at various points along the way. During the day they slept, exhausted.

The Colonel and Sergeant Tibs nervously paced the floor of their stable. "What has happened to them?" said the Colonel. "They should have been here by now."

A long red and black car, driven like the wind, shot down the nearby road and screeched to a stop in front of Hell Hall.

"Blast it all," grumbled the Colonel. "Better see what's up, Tibs. On the double, man! On the double!" Tibs jumped on the Colonel's back, and the two started once again plowing through the snow drifts toward the forbidding mansion.

Tibs chose his old route of entry, and got to the living room door just in time to hear Cruella De Vil say to the Baduns,

"I've got no time to argue! I tell you, it's got to be done tonight!"

"But the pups ain't big enough," Horace said. "You couldn't get a half dozen coats out of the whole kaboodle!"

Sergeant Tibs was aghast.

"Coats—dog-skin coats!" he groaned. "So that's it!"

"Now listen," shouted Cruella, "I'll be back in the morning—and the job had better be done. Do you understand?" With a great slam of the door, she was gone.

Tibs squeezed himself through a hole next to the door and nudged the nearest puppies.

"You'd better get out of here if you want to save your skins," he whispered. "There's a hole in the wall—there by the door. Come on. Shake a leg."

Luckily, Horace and Jasper were absorbed in their favorite television show. Otherwise they would surely have seen the procession of puppies that squeezed, one by one, through the small hole.

Tibs ran from end to end of the line, trying to keep the puppies in order. "Faster! Faster!" he urged. "One at a time!"

Pushing and squeezing and struggling, the

pups got through the hole. The television show was almost at an end. At any moment the Baduns might look around and discover them.

Finally, the last pup in the line scrambled through to safety. But no, there was still one left! Tibs groaned as he saw him, sitting right in front of the television set, watching the show.

How was he to reach him without warning Horace and Jasper?

Tibs' problem was solved when Jasper disgustedly picked up the puppy and tossed him out of the way.

Tibs grabbed the puppy and frantically tried to squeeze him through the hole, just as the television show ended.

The hole was small, and the puppy was large, and he couldn't help giving out a little yip as Tibs struggled to force him through.

"Hey! Horace—look!" shouted Jasper, as he turned around and saw the empty room. "The pups are gone! They flew the coop! Right out through that little hole—there! Grab a flashlight!"

Jasper grabbed a poker from the fireplace, and the two Baduns burst into the hallway.

Behind them, up the stairs, the puppies were just turning the corner. But the last puppy slipped on the top stair, bounced down a step and yipped in surprise.

"There they go,—up the stairs," shouted Jasper.

The puppies were nowhere to be seen.

"Here, puppies," said Jasper coaxingly. "Come here, now. Don't go hiding from your old Uncle Jasper. I won't hurt you."

"But I thought we were going to pop them off," said Horace.

"Shhh!" admonished Jasper. "Shut up! Take a squint in that room and I'll take these other two rooms."

Sergeant Tibs had herded the puppies under an enormous bed, but he knew that they wouldn't be safe for long. Jasper burst into the room, and the bright beam of his flashlight suddenly lit up their hiding place. To Jasper, it seemed that there was a veritable explosion of small dogs, as Tibs and the puppies knocked him off his feet and stampeded over him.

"It's that mangy tabby cat!" cried the infuriated Jasper. "He's the ring leader. Head them off, Horace—head them off!"

Tibs and the puppies raced down the stairs. The Colonel, watching outside a window, blinked as he saw the stream of puppies with the Baduns in close pursuit. "I say, Sergeant, wait a moment!" he called.

"No time to explain!" shouted Tibs as he dashed past. Then he added politely, "Sorry, sir. Busy, sir."

It was just at this moment that Pongo and Perdita, after a long and wearisome journey, hesitated at the crossroads. Perdita was discouraged. "Pongo, Pongo," she wailed. "I'm afraid we're lost."

"I don't think so, Perdy. It can't be far," said Pongo. Once more he barked the alert message. The Colonel heard it.

"By Jove," he exclaimed. "It's the Pongos —at last!"

He raced out to meet them.

"Are—are you the Colonel?" asked Pongo. "Our puppies? Are they all right?"

"No time to explain," answered the old sheepdog. "I'm afraid there's trouble. Big hullaballoo. Come along. Follow me."

The three hurried off towards Hell Hall.

The Colonel was right. There *was* trouble.

Tibs and the puppies were backed up in a corner, and the Baduns were standing menacingly over them.

Jasper was jubilant. "Ha!" he gloated. "Now we got them, Horace. They've finally run out of room. Now we can do the job."

But before either of them could land a blow, there was a crash of splintering glass as Pongo and Perdita leaped through a window into the room.

The Baduns whirled around in surprise.

"Hey, what's this!" cried Jasper. Then he gave a bellow as Pongo made a flying leap for his leg.

"Looks like a couple of spotted hyenas!" croaked Horace.

There was a wild melee of swinging clubs and flying bodies. The dogs were quicker and more agile than the Baduns, and in the confusion the men landed more blows on each other than on the Dalmatians. But Jasper connected with a lucky kick, and Pongo crashed into the door, where he lay dazed.

"There, you mangy mongrel!" shouted Jasper. "I'll knock your blinking block off!" He swung his heavy poker, but a bite from Perdita spoiled his aim, and his blow smashed through the old, crumbling door as Pongo

returned to the fray. The Colonel poked his head through the hole.

"Go on, Tibs!" he thundered. "Give them what for!"

"No, Colonel, no!" panted Tibs, seeing a way of escape. "Retreat! Retreat!"

The Colonel saw immediately that Tibs was right, for the fight in the room was growing wilder by the minute.

"Yes, yes! Retreat!" the old sheepdog agreed.

Quick as a cat, Tibs herded the puppies through the broken door, and the long line of them floundered through the drifts on their way to the Captain's stable.

There was no doubt about it, the Baduns were getting the worst of the fight. Perdita pulled a rug from under Horace, who fell into the smouldering fireplace. He emerged, shrieking, and collided with Jasper. The two landed against the wall, the ancient house shook, and the villains were bombarded with a shower of falling plaster.

"Come on, Perdy Let's go," said Pongo, and the two dashed after the trail of the puppies as the Baduns struggled to get out of the debris that covered them.

Jasper shook himself, furious. "I'll skin every one of those little spotted fiends, if it's the last thing I do."

The Colonel, Sergeant Tibs and all the Dalmatians had vanished, but their trail led unmistakably over the hill to the Captain's stable. Arming themselves with poker and chair leg, the Baduns ran to their truck.

REUNION

It was a warm reunion in the stable, with all the fifteen puppies talking at once, and Perdita and Pongo were abrim with delight.

"All fifteen here?" anxiously asked Pongo.

"More than twice that many, lad," said Lucky. "Now there are ninety-nine!"

"Uh—ni—*ninety-nine!*" stuttered Pongo. He and Perdita stared aghast at the sea of Dalmatian puppies that filled the stable. "What on earth would Cruella De Vil want with so many?"

"She was going to make *coats* out of us," blurted out one puppy. Pongo and Perdita were shocked into silence. Sergeant Tibs affirmed the puppy's startling news. "That's right!" he said solemnly. "*Dog-skin* coats."

The kindly old Colonel huffed and spluttered. "Oh, come now, Tibs! Dog-skin coats, indeed. I don't believe it!"

Sergeant Tibs stood his ground. "It's true, sir," the cat insisted. "I heard the Baduns and Cruella talking about it at Hell Hall."

Pongo and Perdita stood perplexed, their fifteen puppies gathered about them in a circle. The other puppies in the room waited and listened anxiously.

"Cruella's a devil—a witch!" cried Perdita. "Oh, Pongo, what will we do?"

"We have to get back to London somehow," Pongo said. "And we'll have to take the other puppies, too, Perdy. *All* of them. Our human pets would never turn them out."

The big horse, Captain, turned from his vantage point by the window. "Colonel, sir," he said. "Lights on the road. It's a truck headed this way." The Colonel bristled.

"It's the Baduns . . . Horace and Jasper," he said. "They're following our tracks." He drew himself to his full height. "Well," he thundered, "we've got them out-numbered, Tibs! When I give the signal, we'll attack!"

Sergeant Tibs saluted respectfully. "Oh, Colonel, sir, I'm afraid that would be disastrous, sir."

"He's right, Colonel," said Pongo. "We'd better make a run for it."

"Better be off," urged the Captain, from his post at the window. "Here they come."

"Thank you, Sergeant, Colonel, Captain. Bless you all," said Perdita. "How can we possibly repay you for everything you've done?"

"It was nothing," said the Colonel gruffly. "All in the line of duty, you know."

The headlights of the approaching Baduns' truck drew nearer, and the puppies, led by Perdita, filed out of the back door and across the pasture. Pongo drew up the rear.

"Good luck, Pongos," called Sergeant Tibs and the Captain.

"Yes. Good luck," added the Colonel, as he watched Horace and Jasper advance from their truck. "Don't worry. We'll hold the Baduns to the bitter end."

Growling, the shaggy old dog confronted the two men at the stable door. Dodging the blows hurled at him by Horace and Jasper, he retreated slowly and grudgingly into the stable's dark interior. The Baduns stared, amazed. There was no sign of the Dalmatians. The Colonel had held the men back long enough for the Pongos and the throng of youngsters to make their escape.

Now it was the Captain's turn to further delay the Baduns. The hoofs of the big horse shot out, and Horace sailed through the air and crashed through the stable wall.

"Splendid, Captain!" shouted Tibs. "Now for the other one!" With a second flash of his hoofs, the old horse booted Jasper across the stable to join his companion. But as Jasper picked himself up out of the snow, he saw the wide trail of dog tracks that led over the hill.

"Hey, there they go, the little sneaks!" he yelped. "Come on, Horace. Back to the truck. We'll head them off in half a mile."

Pongo realized their tracks in the snow would be easy to follow, and he was worried. But suddenly luck fell in their way—a frozen creek. Its smooth, icy surface would leave no sign of their passing. Slipping and sliding, he and Perdita herded their floundering group onto the ice. They gained the safety of the underside of a stone bridge just as the pursuing Baduns pulled their truck to a stop on the road overhead. One pup skidded almost into the Baduns' view, but Pongo pulled it back to safety. They could hear Jasper and Horace talking:

"Jasper, I've been thinking. What if those dogs went down the frozen creek so as not to leave their tracks?"

"Aw, Horace, you idiot!" retorted Jasper. "Dogs aren't that smart!" With a grinding of gears, the truck went on. Pongo waited until it had disappeared from view.

"All clear, Perdy," he announced, and they continued their slipping, sliding progress. The puppies were having a difficult time keeping their feet, and some wanted to desert the icy creek for the snowy banks. But Pongo was firm.

"If we leave tracks, we're done for," he said. They went on into the night.

DOGS IN BLACK SUITS

It began to snow, and at last Pongo decided that it was safe to abandon the slippery ice and strike across country. Perdita still led the line of marching puppies, and Pongo counted them as they trudged on past . . . Ninety-nine! Where was Lucky? Pongo retraced his steps to find the puppy.

"I'm tired," wailed Lucky, "and I'm hungry, and my tail's froze. And my nose is froze, and my toes are froze."

Pongo picked him up by the collar and hurried after the others. He was worried, for the snow was coming down faster and he was afraid they had lost their way. Then he heard a short bark, and a magnificent collie appeared through the swirling snow flakes.

"Pongo! Pongo!" he called. "Thank goodness. We had just about lost hope. We have shelter for you at the dairy barn across the way."

They followed the collie through a fence and up a hill into the warmth of the barn. Pleasant-faced, brown-eyed cows gazed in astonishment at them.

"Just look, Queenie," said one. "Have you ever seen so many adorable puppies? Poor dears! They're completely worn out and half frozen."

Some of the puppies started to whimper. After all, they were small and they'd come a long way through cold and snow. Also, they had had nothing to eat for hours. "I'm hungry, mother," said one to Perdita.

"I'm sorry, children . . ." Perdita started to say, when one of the cows interrupted her: "Wouldn't your children like some warm fresh milk?" she said.

"Oh, thank you," said Perdita gratefully. Soon each hungry pup had been fed. Then one by one, the puppies dropped off to sleep. The collie brought scraps of food for the weary Pongo and Perdita.

"Not much, but it might hold you as far as Dinsford. There's a Labrador there. His pet is a grocer. I'll head you that way in the morning."

While the weary Dalmatians slept, the collie stood guard. In the morning, greatly refreshed, the Pongos thanked their generous hosts, and went on their way. The storm had ended, and the countryside was now covered with a new blanket of gleaming snow. Pongo knew that their tracks would show plainly in the snow. He headed the army of pups towards the wooded countryside, where they would be better hidden.

Still, occasionally they had to cross a road, and Pongo would look searchingly up and down its length before sending the puppies across. Once they were safely on the other side, Pongo would draw a broken branch back and forth over the road to wipe out the tell-tale tracks.

The prints of one little puppy's feet do not leave marks too noticeable in fresh-fallen snow. But multiply those prints by ninety-nine, add the larger prints of two grown dogs, and you have a track difficult to erase. Pongo was trying to obliterate their tracks across a snowy road when a speeding red and black car loomed into view.

It was Cruella De Vil, who had now entered the chase, and was being closely followed by the Baduns in their rickety truck. The dogs had fled, but Cruella spotted the tracks across the road and the car screeched to a stop.

"Well, now," she exulted. "What have we

here! So they thought they could outwit Cruella! Ha! Ha!" Turning to the Baduns' truck she shouted: "Jasper! Horace! Here are their tracks, heading straight for the village. Work your way south on the side roads. I'll take the main road. See you in Dinsford." With a clashing and grinding of gears, the two machines drove off.

Pongo, Perdita and the puppies were running as fast as they could toward the sound of distant barking. It came from the Dinsford Labrador, who came racing up with excellent news.

"Pongo," he barked. "I've got a ride home for all of you, if we can make it. Come on. We'd better hurry!"

The black Labrador led them through back ways into a deserted blacksmith shop. "It's dark in here," whispered one pup. "And scary!" added another. "And it's dirty!" said a third. But, temporarily, it was shelter and a hiding place. The Labrador nodded toward a broken window.

"See that van down the street?" he said. "It's going to London as soon as the engine's repaired. And there's room for all of you."

As the three looked through the broken pane, a long red and black car flashed into the street and skidded to a stop.

"Pongo, look!" said Perdita. "There's Cruella!"

"Yes," said Pongo, "and here come Horace and Jasper." The Baduns' truck clanked to a shuddery stop. Impatiently, Cruella sat in her car while Horace and Jasper emerged and began searching the small village street.

"How will we ever get to the van?" said Perdita.

"I don't know, Perdy," answered Pongo. "But—somehow—we've got to."

Cruella De Vil, impatient at the delay in finding the Dalmatians, drove slowly up and down the street to carry on her own search. The Baduns were still combing alleys for signs of the dogs, and might return at any moment. How was Pongo to get his swarm of puppies into the van? As he pondered on the problem, two of the puppies tumbled out of the fireplace.

"Mother! Dad!" cried one. "Patch pushed me into the soot."

"Lucky pushed me first," said Patch. Both puppies were half-covered with coal-dust and hardly recognizable. Pongo stared at them. Then he turned to Perdita: "I've got an idea!" he said. Before Perdita's amazed eyes he jumped into the fireplace and rolled about in the soot.

"Pongo! What on earth . . ." began Perdita, horrified. Then Pongo emerged from the soot cloud he'd been raising. He was as black as their friend, the Labrador.

"Look!" he cried. "I'm a *Labrador!* We'll *all* roll in the soot. We'll *all* be Labradors, and, if we travel in small groups. . . ."

Perdita was frightened, and a little dubious. Besides, she hated to spoil her gleaming white coat. "I'm afraid we can't fool Cruella," she said.

"We can try," said Pongo. "Into the soot, children!"

"You mean you want us to get dirty?" asked Lucky. The puppies couldn't believe their ears. But a nod of assent from Perdita sent them rolling and tumbling in the sooty fireplace, and a great cloud of soot rose up.

The Labrador was heartily in favor of the plan. He rather liked the idea of seeing a hundred and one black Labradors. "I'll take the first bunch of puppies to the van," he said. "Then I'll stay there and haul the rest of them aboard. You follow me with little groups."

The Pongos waited and watched apprehensively at the window as the Labrador led the first puppies to the back of the van.

"Pongo," said Perdita. "I'm so afraid."

Pongo gave her a reassuring lick. "Don't worry, Perdy. It won't be long now. Soon we'll be home."

The line of black puppies passed by Horace, who stopped and looked at them in puzzlement. He plucked at Jasper's sleeve. "Look, Jasper. Do you suppose those Dalmatians have disguised themselves?"

"Oh, yes, Horace," answered Jasper sarcastically. "That's *just* what they did! Dogs are *always* painting themselves black. You idiot!" Jasper thumped Horace soundly over the head and scrambled over the nearest fence to continue his search.

It was Pongo's turn to load more puppies aboard the van. "So far, so good," he told Perdita. "I'll go ahead with the next bunch. You follow as soon as all mine are in. The van may leave at any minute."

Pongo and the Labrador frantically loaded black puppies into the van. Cruella De Vil had returned in her big car and now was screeching at the Baduns:

"They're somewhere in this village and we're going to find them! Now—get going!" The Baduns, grumbling, continued their search, while Cruella sat in her car and fidgeted nervously. Past her came another

file of black puppies, headed by an equally black Perdita.

The van's motor had started.

"There," said the mechanic to the truck driver. "That ought to do her. At least, she'll get you back to London." It was time for haste. Perdita helped the Labrador load puppies onto the van's tailgate.

"Better get aboard, ma'am," said the Labrador as Pongo raced back toward the blacksmith shop to get the last of the puppies.

"Come on, children," cried Pongo. "Run on ahead." He felt apprehensive, for between them and the safety of the van sat Cruella, watching the puppies suspiciously.

"Keep going! Keep going!" Pongo urged the pups. It was unfortunate that just as the last one, Lucky, passed under the eaves, some melting snow fell onto his back. Dripping off, it exposed the puppy's white hide and spotted markings. Cruella's suspicions had been confirmed!

"It can't be!" she shouted. "It's impossible! Horace! Jasper! Come here!"

The Baduns came on the run, but the van was already on the move, and Pongo was bounding after it with the last pup in his mouth. Perdita, on the tailgate, urged them on. Desperately, Pongo leaped for the truck, and Perdita, with a frantic grab for his collar, pulled him and the puppy to safety.

"There they go! In the van! After them!" screeched Cruella. But the black Labrador cunningly tripped the Baduns, and, before they could disentangle themselves, the van had turned the corner and was speeding along on its way to London.

THE CHASE

The van was big and roomy, and partly filled with furniture. For the first time in days Pongo and Perdita felt secure. The van driver sped along, for it was Christmas Eve, and he was anxious to get home.

"Perdy, we made it," exulted Pongo. "Just think—we'll all be home tonight." He started to sing a cheerful song:

"Soon we'll be seeing the sights of London.
Once we're there we'll never leave.
Give three cheers, a yip and a bark,
We'll be back in Regents Park,
This jolly Christmas Eve.
London is just around the corner . . ."

Suddenly the headlights of a speeding car lit up the interior of the van.

"Pongo! It's her! Cruella!" cried Perdita. The pups, frightened by the glaring lights, dived into dresser drawers and boxes. Cruella put her foot on the gas and began to overtake the van. By maneuvering her car to left and right, she hoped to be able to force the van into the ditch.

"Hey, lady! What on earth are you trying to do?" yelled the van driver, as he fought to keep his position on the slippery road.

"You crazy woman driver! Move over!"

Pongo and Perdita, inside the jolting, swaying van, desperately tried to keep their feet. The terrified puppies were safely hidden in the furniture. They could only hold on and try to ride out this mad race.

It was Horace and Jasper who decided the issue. Speeding behind Cruella's car, they had seen her attempts to ditch the van. Jasper now decided that Fate lay in his capable hands.

"Watch, Horace," he gloated. "There's nothing to it. I'll give them a bit of a nudge . . . Ha! Ha! Ha! . . . and shove them into the ditch." Jasper urged the rickety old truck to greater speed.

"Watch out, Perdy," said Pongo, as the van, the Baduns' truck and Cruella's huge car drew closer together on the narrow slippery surface of the road.

The van driver was in no mood to be delayed. He was overdue at his home in London, and the Christmas tree was waiting to be trimmed. No wild-eyed women in big cars or men in rusty trucks were going to stop *him*.

He clung to his steering wheel and continued his lively pace to London, dodging now and then to avoid the batterings of Cruella and the Baduns. Such reckless maneuverings couldn't continue forever.

Suddenly there was a bang and a slam as the Baduns, trying to ditch the van, bumped into Cruella's car. Pieces of metal showered the roadway and the van teetered precariously. But it recovered and continued on its way. Left behind in the snowy ditch were Cruella and her villainous henchmen.

"You *fools!* You *imbeciles!* You *idiots!*" she screeched.

Horace and Jasper had reached the end of their endurance. Slowly they picked themselves out of the remains of their smashed truck, and faced Cruella with whatever dignity two such low fellows could muster.

"That's enough!" they said in unison, and started to trudge down the road.

Cruella De Vil, standing in the wreckage of her expensive car, looked at the damage she had caused. Her arrogant shoulders fell and her once-proud features were twisted with tearful rage. Cruella De Vil, meanest girl in London, had given up.

HOME FOR CHRISTMAS

It was Christmas Eve in the Radcliff's little home in Regents Park, but nobody was feeling particularly cheerful. Anita was bravely putting the last touches on the Christmas tree, and Roger was listening moodily to the radio. To the accompaniment of a famous orchestra, someone was singing Roger's hit tune:

"At first you think Cruella is a devil,
But after time has worn away the shock,

You come to realize
You've seen her kind of eyes
Watching you from underneath a rock.
Cruella De Vil. . . .
Cruella De Vil. . . ."

Snap! Roger had turned off the set. Anita looked up from where she knelt by the tree.

"Don't you want to listen, Roger? After all, it *is* your first big song hit."

"I know," said Roger gloomily. He walked over to a photograph of Pongo and Perdita, and looked at it for a long time. Anita came and stood silently by his side. "I still can't believe it, Anita," he said. " . . . that Pongo and Perdita would run away."

"Here's a bit of Christmas cheer for you," said Nanny Cook, bustling in from the kitchen with a tray. Then she saw them looking at the picture. "Oh, the dear little puppies . . . sniff . . . sometimes at night I can hear them barking. But it always turns out I'm dreaming."

Dabbing her apron to her eyes, Nanny turned to go back to the kitchen. Suddenly there came a loud barking at the front door. Nanny stood stock still, then she whirled about, and, almost knocking Roger over in her mad dash past him, ran down the tiny hall and opened the door.

An avalanche of black, happy, barking dogs swarmed over Nanny as she opened the door. Knocked off her feet, the little maid lay there while some of the dogs licked her face and pranced about with glee. The rest of the canine throng streamed into the living room.

Roger was completely overpowered by the wave of happy animals, and Anita was pushed to the sofa by two of the largest.

She wasn't frightened, but she *was* a little startled.

"Roger," she cried. "What on earth . . . ?"

Roger tried to regain his feet. "Why—they're Labradors," he said.

"No—no!" cried Nanny happily, as she came running into the room. "They're Dalmatians covered with soot! Look!" She picked up a black-and-white spotted pup from the mass on the floor. "Look, here's Lucky!"

"Oh, Pongo boy—is that you?" said Roger. He pulled a handkerchief from his pocket and dabbed at the big dog's head. The soot came off, and there stood Pongo, familiar in his handsome white coat and black spots.

"Pongo! It's Pongo!" sang Roger. He grasped Pongo's paws and the two did a joyful dance around the room.

Anita, almost smothered by fond licking on her face and hands, was trying to wipe soot off the other big dog. "Perdy—oh, Perdy, my darling. You've come back!"

Nanny Cook was busy with her feather duster. "And Patch," she said, as another familiar puppy emerged from his sooty coat. "And Rolly and Penny and Freckles—oh, ho, ho! They're all here, the little dears!"

Roger hugged Anita close to him. "It's a miracle," he said.

"Yes," smiled Anita. "Oh, Rog—what a wonderful Christmas present."

Pongo and Perdita looked at each other happily. They—and the puppies—were home at last.

A DALMATIAN PLANTATION

Nanny Cook continued to wield her feather duster. Clouds of soot filled the room, and dozens of coughing, spluttering, dusty, but unmistakably black and white, spotted puppies emerged. Nanny turned to the Radcliffs, who were still happily absorbed in their own cluster of dogs.

"Did you notice," she said, "there are a lot more of them."

Roger and Anita looked. And then they blinked in utter disbelief. The room was literally overflowing with puppies—dozens and dozens of Dalmatian puppies!

They crowded on the top of the piano, spilled over onto the keyboard, and from there onto the bench. The window seat was full of them, and so were all the chairs. The coffee table was covered.

Dalmatian pups swarmed over the sofa. Puppies thronged the hall. A few had found their way to the fireplace mantel to avoid the crowd on the floor. And all the way up the stairs to the second floor landing, puppies sat patiently waiting while Nanny Cook as patiently dusted.

"Look, Anita," exclaimed Roger. "Puppies everywhere. There must be a hundred!"

Nanny was dusting and counting: "One, two, three, and four is seven . . ." Roger and Anita joined in. "Two, four, six . . . and three makes nine more."

Eleven puppies were discovered under the curtains by the window, and Anita found quite a number under the Christmas tree.

A closer search revealed one in the fire-place, and finally Roger said, "Let's see now. That's eighty-four! Add our *fifteen* puppies, plus Pongo and Perdita . . . and we have ONE HUNDRED AND ONE DALMA-TIANS! Oh, ho, Pongo . . . what an old rascal you are!" He rubbed the big dog's head. "Where did they all come from?"

Anita sank onto the sofa. "What will we do with all of them?" she said.

Nanny had finished dusting the last puppy. She turned now to hear what Roger would say. Pongo and Perdita looked at each other apprehensively. The puppies looked at Roger, and tremblingly awaited his answer.

Roger looked at the floor.

Finally he looked up, to meet the gaze of one hundred and one pairs of anxious eyes. Roger smiled—a big, warm, happy smile. "We'll *keep* them," he said simply.

Pongo and Perdita sighed with relief. The warm hearts of their human pets hadn't disappointed them. The puppies wriggled and barked and wagged their tails.

"Keep all one hundred and one—in this little house?" gasped Anita, over the din.

"We'll buy a big place in the country," answered Roger. "We'll have a *plantation*—er —a *Dalmatian plantation.*"

"Oh, Roger," smiled Anita. She hugged him and added, "That's truly an inspiration."

"It'll be a sensation!" laughed Nanny, and turned to dust one puppy that she somehow had missed.

Roger picked his way through the happy, squirming dogs to the piano and began to improvise:

"We'll have a Dalmatian plantation—
*   a Dalmatian plantation, I say.*
A life-long vacation . . .
*   complete resignation*
To sweet relaxation and play.
Our new population is no complication . . ."

Anita interrupted: "And we do have enough money."

"No, no!" said Roger. "Remuneration!" He finished the song:

"We'll have a Dalmatian plantation,
Where our population can roam.
In this location, our whole aggregation
Will love our plantation home."

And if you ever go to a certain place in England, you can still see those dogs today, in their plantation home, happily roaming its woods and fields—the one hundred and one Dalmatians.

UNCLE REMUS STORIES

Johnny and Uncle Remus were friends. Johnny's hair was brown, his skin was fair, and he was not quite nine. Uncle Remus' hair was white, his skin was black, and no one knew how old he was.

The house where Johnny lived had everything—big rooms, big doors, big doorknobs, big chairs, big windows that looked out on the family's fields of cotton, tobacco, and corn. The cabin where Uncle Remus lived had almost nothing at all, just one little room where Uncle Remus slept and cooked and smoked his corncob pipe. His only window looked out through the trees toward a swamp.

The reason Johnny loved Uncle Remus so much was the wonderful things that he knew. He knew everything there was to know about the birds, the animals, and all the creatures. He even understood the language they used when they spoke; he understood what the Screech-Owl said to the Hoot-Owl in the tree outside his cabin; he understood *I-doom-er-ker-kum-mer-ker*, the Turtle talk, that bubbled up from the bottom of the creek.

Johnny liked to hear Uncle Remus tell stories about what the creatures were doing, and he liked the funny old-fashioned way he spoke. Every evening before supper, he and his friend Ginny went down to Uncle Remus' cabin to listen. All Uncle Remus had to do was to take one puff on his pipe, and a story would just start rolling out with the smoke. It might be a story about a Lion, an Elephant, or a Bullfrog; but most of the stories were about that smartest of all little creatures, Brer Rabbit, and the tricks that he played on Brer Fox and Brer Bear.

"An der will never be an end ter de stories about Brer Rabbit," said Uncle Remus to Ginny, "cause he's always up ter somethin' new. Brer Rabbit, he ain't very big; he ain't very strong; but when dat thinkin' machine of his starts cookin' up devilment, he's de smartest creetur on dis earf."

DE TAR-BABY

One day, Brer Fox and Brer Bear wuz sittin' round in de woods, talkin' about de way Brer Rabbit wuz always cuttin' up capers an actin' so fresh.

"Brer Rabbit's gettin' much too sassy," say Brer Fox to de Brer Bear.

"Brer Rabbit's gettin' much too bossy," say Brer Bear to de Brer Fox.

"Brer Rabbit don't mind his own bizness," say Brer Fox.

"Brer Rabbit talk much too biggity," say Brer Bear to de Brer Fox.

"I don't like de way Brer Rabbit go prancin' *lippity clippity lippity clippity* down de road," say Brer Bear.

"Some day I'm goin' ter ketch Brer Rabbit an pull out his mustarshes, *pripp! propp! pripp! propp!*" say Brer Fox.

"Some day I'm goin' ter ketch Brer Rabbit an knock his head clean off, *blim, blam! blim, blam!*" say Brer Bear.

Right den, Brer Fox get a powerful big idea. "I'm goin' ter ketch Brer Rabbit *now*."

Well suh, Brer Fox went straight ter wurk. First, he got some tar. Den, he make it inter a shape, sorter like a baby, wid arms and legs, a stummock, an a head. "Now," he say, "we got ter make dis Tar-Baby look real." Wid dat, he pull some hairs, *plip! plip!* right outer Brer Bear's back, and stick um on de Tar-Baby's head. He snatch off Brer Bear's yellow hat an his own blue coat, an he put

um on de Tar-Baby. "Come now, Brer Bear, help me carry dis Tar-Baby ter de big road wher Brer Rabbit's sure ter come."

Dey took de Tar-Baby, and dey sot him down under a tree at de side of de road, sorter like he mighter been restin'. Den, Brer Fox and Brer Bear lay down in de bushes ter wait fer Brer Rabbit.

Dey didn't have ter wait long. Purty soon, dey heard a whistlin' an a hummin', an along come Brer Rabbit, prancin' *lippity clippity,* sassy ez a mockin' bird. All 't once, he spy de Tar-Baby.

"Howdy!" sing out Brer Rabbit.

De Tar-Baby, he say nothin', an Brer Fox and Brer Bear, dey lay low in de bushes an dey say nothin'.

Brer Rabbit wait fer de Tar-Baby ter answer. Den he say, louder dan before, "What's de matter wid you? I said *howdy do.* Is you deaf? If you is, I can holler louder."

De Tar-Baby, he say nothin', an Brer Fox and Brer Bear, dey lay low.

Den Brer Rabbit holler real loud, at de Tar-Baby, loud ez he can. "Wher's your politeness? Ain't you goin' ter say *howdy do*

like respectubble folks say when dey meet up on de road?"

De Tar-Baby, he say nothin', an Brer Fox and Brer Bear, dey lay low.

Now Brer Rabbit sorter mad. He clinch his fist and he walk right up close ter de Tar-Baby. "If you don't say *howdy do* by de time I count three, I'm goin' ter *blip* you in de nose." Now de Brer Rabbit he start countin', "One, two, . . ."

But de Tar-Baby, he say nothin', an Brer Fox and Brer Bear, dey just wink der eyes an grin an dey lay low.

"Three!" yell Brer Rabbit. Now he mighty mad. He draw back his right fist, and *blip!* he hit de Tar-Baby smack in de nose. But Brer Rabbit's right fist stuck der in de tar. Brer Rabbit he can't pull it loose.

Now Brer Rabbit turrible mad. "Let go my fist!" he holler. Wid dat, he draw back his other fist, and *blip!* again he hit de Tar-Baby smack in de nose. But dis fist stuck der in de tar too. He can't pull it loose.

De Tar-Baby, he say nothin', and Brer Fox and Brer Bear dey sorter chuckle in der stummocks an dey lay low.

"If you don't let go my fists," holler Brer Rabbit, "I'm goin' ter kick your teef right outer your mouf!"

Well suh, Brer Rabbit kicked. First he pull back one behind foot, an *pow!* he hit de Tar-Baby in de jaw. But Brer Rabbit's behind foot stuck der in de tar. Den he pull back de other behind foot. Den, *pow!* Brer Rabbit hit de Tar-Baby in de stummock wid de behind foot. Dis foot stuck der in de tar too.

"If you don't let go my behind foots," squall out Brer Rabbit to de Tar-Baby, "I'm goin' ter butt you wid my head till you ain't got no bref left in your body!"

Brer Rabbit butted, but his head stuck der in de tar. Now Brer Rabbit's two fists, his two behind foots, an his head wuz all stuck in de Tar-Baby. He push an he pull, but de more he try ter get unstuck-up, de stucker-up he got. Soon Brer Rabbit is so stuck up he can't skacely move his eyeballs.

Now Brer Fox an Brer Bear come outer de bushes, an dey feel mighty good. Dey dance round an round Brer Rabbit, laffin' and hollerin' fit ter kill.

"We sure ketched you dis time, Brer Rabbit," say Brer Bear.

"You better say your prayers, Brer Rabbit," say Brer Fox to him, "cause dis is de very last day of your life."

Brer Rabbit, he shiver an trimble, cause he wuz in a mighty bad fix, an he wuz mighty skeered of de Brer Fox and de Brer Bear. But right den Brer Rabbit set his mind aworkin' how ter get hisself outer dat fix real quick.

"Brer Rabbit," say Brer Bear, "you been bouncin' round dis neighborhood bossin' everybody fer a long time. Now I'm de boss, an I'm goin' ter knock your head clean off."

"No," say Brer Fox. "Dat's too easy an too quick. We got ter make him suffer."

"Brer Rabbit," he say, "you been sassin' me, stickin' your head inter my bizness fer years an years. Now I got you. I'm goin' ter

fix up a great big fire. Den, when it's good an hot, I'm goin' ter drop you in an roast you, right here dis very day."

Now Brer Rabbit ain't really skeered any more, cause he got an idea how he goin' ter get loose. But he talk like he's de most skeered rabbit in all dis wurld. "I don't care what you do wid me," he say, pretendin' ter shake an quake all over, "just so you don't fling me over dese bushes into dat brier-patch. Roast me just ez hot ez you please, but don't fling me in dat brier-patch!"

"Hold on a minute," say Brer Bear, tappin' Brer Fox on de shoulder. "It's goin' ter be a lot of trouble ter roast Brer Rabbit. Furst, we'll have ter fetch a big pile of kindlin' wood. Den we'll have ter make de big fire."

Brer Fox scratch his head. "Dat's so. Well den, Brer Rabbit, I'm goin' ter hang you."

"Hang me just ez high ez you please," say Brer Rabbit to Brer Fox, "but please don't fling me in dat brier-patch!"

"It's goin' ter be a lot of trouble ter hang Brer Rabbit," say Brer Bear. "Furst, we'll have ter fetch a big long rope."

"Dat's so," say Brer Fox. "Well den, Brer Rabbit, I'm goin' ter drown you."

"Drown me just ez deep ez you please," say Brer Rabbit, "but please, *please* don't fling me in dat brier-patch!"

"It's goin' ter be a lot of trouble ter drown Brer Rabbit," say Brer Bear. "Furst, we'll have ter carry him way down to de river."

"Dat's so," say Brer Fox. "Well, Brer Rabbit, I expect de best way is ter skin you. Come on, Brer Bear, let's get started."

"Skin me," say Brer Rabbit, "pull out my ears, snatch off my legs an chop off my tail, but please, *please*, PLEASE, Brer Fox an Brer Bear, don't fling me in dat brier-patch!"

Now Brer Bear sorter grumble. "Wait a minute, Brer Fox. It ain't goin' ter be much fun ter skin Brer Rabbit, cause he ain't skeered of bein' skinned."

"But he sure is skeered of dat brier-patch!" say Brer Fox. "An dat's just wher he's goin' ter go! Dis is de end of Brer Rabbit!" Wid dat, he yank Brer Rabbit off de Tar-Baby and he fling him, *kerblam!* right inter de middle of de brier-patch.

Well suh, der wuz a considerabul flutter in de place where Brer Rabbit struck dose brier bushes. *"Ooo! Oow! Ouch!"* he yell. He screech an he squall! De ruckus an de hullabaloo wuz awful. Den, by-m-by, de *Ooo!* and de *Oow!* an de *Ouch!* come only in a weak tired whisper.

Brer Fox and Brer Bear, dey listen an grin. Den dey shake hands an dey slap each other on de back.

"Brer Rabbit ain't goin' ter be sassy no more!" say de Brer Fox.

"Brer Rabbit ain't goin' ter be bossy no more!" say de Brer Bear.

"Brer Rabbit ain't goin' ter do *nothin'* no more!" say de Brer Fox an de Brer Bear.

"Dis is de end! *Brer Rabbit is dead!*"

But right den, Brer Fox and Brer Bear hear a scufflin' mongst de leaves, way at de other end of de brier-patch. And lo an behold, who do dey see scramblin' out from de bushes, frisky ez a cricket, but Brer Rabbit hisself! Brer Rabbit, whistlin' an singin' an combin' de last bit of tar outer his mustarshes wid a piece of de brier-bush!

"Howdy, Brer Fox an Brer Bear!" he holler. "I told you an told you not to fling me in dat brier-patch. Dat's de place in all dis world I love de very best. Dat brier-patch is de place wher I wuz born!"

Wid dat, he prance away, *lippity-clippity*, laffin' an laffin' till he can't laff no more.

DE WULLER-DE-WUST

"I'm tired of eatin' cabbiges," say Brer Rabbit one mawnin'. "An I'm tired of carrots, sparrer-grass an beans. I'd like ter sink my teef in somethin' sweet." Wid dat, he took a notion ter run over ter Brer Bear's house, ter see what dey had ter eat over der.

Whiles he wuz lippity-clippitin' along on

his way, lo an behold, who should he meet up wid but Brer Bear hisself. Mrs. Bear wuz strollin' beside him, and shufflin' along right behind wuz der two chilluns, Kubs an Klibs.

"Howdy!" say Brer Rabbit, makin' a bow real perlite.

"Howdy!" say Brer Bear and Mrs. Bear,

bowin' just ez perlite. Den Kubs and Klibs, dey say Howdy, an dey bow too.

Brer Rabbit, he sot down on his hunkers till dey pass by, "Hmmm," he think. "Dat Bear fambly is round an fat ez a dish of butter balls. Dey must have somethin' sweet an tasty in der pantry cubbud, an I'm goin' ter have a lick of it right now."

Now Brer Rabbit take a short cut throo de bushes, an he get ter Brer Bear's house while der ain't nobody der. He walk in de front door an begin a-sniffin' and a-snuffin' round. He peep in here; he poke in der. He nibble a little of dis; he gobble a little of dat. Den all 't once, he spy a bucket of honey, way on a high-up shelf. "Mmmm . . . mmmm!" Brer Rabbit smack his lips. He start scramblin' up, and he make a grab fer dat honeybucket, when—*pow!* it come tumblin' down. It slosh all over him; just a little more an he'd been drowned. From de top of his ears ter de tip of his tail, he wuz just drippin' wid gooey, gluey honey.

Brer Rabbit lick up a big mouffut, an den he ask hisself, "What'll I do now? If I stay in here, Brer Bear'll come back an ketch me. But I'm ashamed ter go outside anywhers, an let de other creeturs see me all stuck-up like dis. Fer massy sake, what *will* I do?"

Well, by-m-by, Brer Rabbit open de door an sneak out. Now of course, de honey make his foots sorter slippery, an de furst thing you know, right der in Brer Bear's front yard, he fall down. He roll over in de leaves. De leaves, dey stick. He kick an scuff dis way an dat ter knock um off, but de more he scuff, de more dey stick. 'Twan't long before he wuz kivvered all over wid leaves. Den he stand up an try ter shake um off, but dey still stick. An wid every shake he make, de leaves, dey go *swishy-swushy, splishy-splushy.* By dis time, Brer Rabbit wuz de skeeriest-lookin', and de skerriest-soundin', creetur you ever laid your eyes on.

Whiles he wuz standin' der, figgerin' out what ter do next, who should happen ter come saunterin' by, but ole Sis Cow. No sooner did she ketch sight of Brer Rabbit in dose leaves dan she set up a howl, an off she gallop, a-mooin' an a-booin' like she seed a ghost.

Brer Rabbit laff.

Now who should come floppin' down outer de air, but Brer Tukkey Buzzard! He take

just one look at Brer Rabbit. Den he flip his wings, an he yank hisself right up inter de air again, screechin' an squallin' till he wuz way up outer sight somewhers in de clouds.

Dis make Brer Rabbit laff some more. He begin ter be mighty pleased about bein' such a skeery-lookin' creetur, an he feel like cuttin' up. Just den, he see Brer Fox come struttin' along, swingin' his fancy walkin'-cane. Brer Rabbit chuckle. He jump out inter de middle of de road, an he give hisself a great big shake . . . *swishy-swushy, splishy-splushy*. Den he kinder sing-song, low an mysterious:

"*I'm de Wuller-de-Wust*
  An You're de One I'm after.
  I think I'll skin you just fer fun—
    You better run,
    You better run,
  Cause I'm de Wuller-de-Wust
  An You're de One I'm after."

Well suh, run wuz just what dat Fox done do. He drop his fancy walkin'-cane an he race off inter de woods. "Oh! Oh, Lawdy! Oh!" he yell, leapin' straight throo de bushes.

Now Brer Rabbit feel so sassy he want ter skeer everybody in de neighborhood. "I'll just wait here an skeer de Bear fambly when dey get back from der walk," he chuckle ter hisself. "I'll skeer um all . . . de whole caboodle." Wid dat, he sot down ter wait in de shade of de tree by Brer Bear's front porch. Purty soon, he got ter feelin' sorter drowsy, an de next thing you know, he dozed off.

Whiles he wuz a-dozin' der in de shade, de sun moved round a bit, till by-m-by Brer Rabbit wuzn't dozin' in de shade no more. He wuz dozin' right in de sizzlin' sun. De sun, it dry up de honey dat wuz kivverin' Brer Rabbit. An de leaves dat wuz stickin' ter de honey dropped off. Now Brer Rabbit don't look like a skeery-creetur no more;

he look just like hisself. But of course, bein' asleep, Brer Rabbit don't know dis.

De furst thing he know, he hear de trompin' of big, heavy foots. Der wuz de Bear fambly, comin' right up toward de porch. Brer Rabbit jump up quick. He leap out from under de tree, an start ter moan:

"I'm de Wuller-de-Wust
  An You're de Ones I'm after.
  I think I'll skin you just fer fun—
    You better run,
    You better run,
  Cause I'm de Wuller-de-Wust
  An You're de Ones I'm after."

De Bear fambly dey stare at Brer Rabbit wid der moufs open wide. Den Brer Bear, he bust out laffin'. "Wuller-de-Wust? What in de name of goodness is de matter wid you, Brer Rabbit? An what's dat dried-up stuff all over you? You're de frowsiest-lookin' creetur I ever did see!"

Brer Rabbit, he look down, an he see dat de leaves dat wuz kivverin' him wuz all gone. An just at dat minute, Brer Bear, he see dat his front door wuz wide open, an dat Brer Rabbit's sticky footprints wuz on de porch.

Brer Bear growl. "Why, you—you—you been messin' round in my honey, you scoundul!" Brer Bear, he reach out an make a grab fer Brer Rabbit. But Brer Bear ain't made ter move very fast, an Brer Rabbit wuz already scootin' outer der, faster dan a streak of lightnin'.

He scooted way off, ter de edge of de river. Den he squot down, an he look at hisself in de water. "Well," he say, "maybe I ain't de skeeriest creetur on dis earf, but I'm de smartest, an de fastest, an I surely have de dried-up honey in de clear, cool water, till purty soon, he wuz all slicked up, like brand new.

PETER AND THE WOLF

FAR UP in the north of Russia, in a cozy cottage at the edge of a great forest, Peter lived with his grandfather.

Peter loved the forest. In summer he roamed its shady paths, visiting his friends the wild animals and birds. He loved the forest in winter, too, when a thick blanket of white snow covered the ground and the frozen lake and clung to the top-most branches of the trees. But in winter Peter could not go into the forest.

"Hungry wolves roam about in the winter," his grandfather told him when he caught Peter trying to steal out. "You must wait until you are old enough to hunt them."

But Peter was certain he was old enough for anything—and too smart for any wolf—right now! So he waited his chance, and when his grandfather dozed, off went Peter, armed with a coil of rope and his own little wooden gun. Down the path he went, ever so quietly, through the gate, across the snowy bridge and into the white forest.

At first Peter felt rather cold and lonely, with whiteness and silence on every side.

Then "Hello, Peter!" twittered a little voice like a flute, and down flew his old friend Sasha, the bird. "What are you doing alone in the forest in the winter?" asked Sasha.

"I'm out to hunt the wolf," said Peter stoutly. "Want to come along?"

Sasha did want to, so on they went together.

Suddenly, on the snowbank ahead, they saw a great threatening shadow. Could it be the wolf?

As Peter and Sasha stood there, quaking, the shadow moved toward them, and out from behind a tree stepped—another old friend of the summer, Sonia, the duck.

"Hello, Sonia," grinned Peter. "We're out to hunt the wolf."

"Oh," said Sonia, "may I come along?"

Of course, Peter and Sasha were glad to have Sonia with them, so she fell into line as they started on again.

But now as they marched along a slinking figure followed them, hidden among the reeds. It was Ivan, the sly cat, who kept hungry eyes on Sonia and Sasha.

As they reached a clearing, pounce! out jumped the cat and sprang at the bird. Only Peter's quick leap saved Sasha from Ivan's jaws.

Peter was shocked.

"Why, Ivan!" he said. "You're a bully!"

Ivan dropped his head guiltily.

"Come on, Sasha," said Peter. "Ivan is sorry. He won't do it again."

With a doubtful glance at Ivan, Sasha hopped back into line.

Once again the brave hunters marched on.

Suddenly, crunch! a lump of snow broke noisily behind them. The line of little hunters spun about.

There was the wolf!

Peter made the leap of his life to a low tree branch. Sasha fluttered up beside Peter on the low tree branch. Ivan scrambled up, too. But Sonia could not fly!

From their hiding places Peter and Sasha and Ivan anxiously watched Sonia scuttle across the snow with the wolf's breath hot upon her. Sonia disappeared from sight behind a fallen log, and they waited, breathless with suspense.

Then the wolf reappeared. And there were duck feathers clinging to his jaws.

Poor Sonia! Poor Sonia! But there was little time for sadness, for the wolf was snarling below Peter, Ivan, and Sasha.

A plan came to Peter! He whispered it to Sasha and Ivan, who twittered and purred their agreement.

First, Sasha flew down from his perch, and flew back and forth in the face of the wolf until the beast was frantic.

Then, down Peter's rope crawled Ivan the cat. Inch by inch Ivan moved closer to where the wolf was battling Sasha.

Ivan crept up behind the angry wolf, with the loop of rope ready for action. Down

went the rope over the wolf's tail! Zing! Ivan pulled the loop tight and Peter, on the bough above, pulled in the slack.

Soon the wolf felt the rope's pull. He reared around, snarling with fresh rage. But Ivan was back on the branch beside Peter, and they were both tugging. They were tugging with every bit of their strength.

There they were, Peter and Ivan, up on their tree branch, and there was the wolf snarling and snapping as he swung by his tail in mid-air.

Now it was Sasha's turn to fly into action again. For off in the forest sounded a hunter's horn. With a tweet of encouragement to his friends, Sasha flew off toward the sound. In and out among the branches he flew until below him he spied three stout hunters marching along.

What could the little bird do to make them follow him? He tried to imitate a wolf howl.

He sputtered and he chirped. Still the hunters did not understand.

"Something must be wrong," said one.

"This little fellow is trying to tell us something," agreed the second.

"Let us take a look," said the third.

So they followed Sasha back to the tree. But what was this? The wolf was snugly bound with the rope, and Peter and Ivan were sitting on him, swinging to and fro.

And who was that coming out from behind the log? It was Sonia, safe and sound, though still a little wobbly on her feet.

And what a gay parade as they entered

the village—Sasha and Ivan and Sonia, and the three hunters carrying the wolf. And at the head of them all, Peter marched proud-ly. Now even his grandfather had to be impressed. For Peter the hunter and his friends had captured the wolf!

THE SLEEPING BEAUTY

ONCE UPON A TIME in a land far away, there lived a handsome king and his fair queen. Their land was at peace and they had many friends. The king and queen should have been perfectly happy in their great castle on the hill.

But, alas, they were not because they had no child. For many years to have a child had been their dearest wish. Then, at last, the wish was granted. A baby daughter was born to them. And so lovely was she, so sweet and full of promise, that they called her Aurora, which means The Dawn.

The day of Aurora's christening was a holiday throughout the kingdom. And everyone, both high and low, was invited to pay homage to the infant princess. It was a day of great joy and celebration.

The streets of the royal city were crowded that morning with happy country folk. They were bringing to the castle their finest fruit, their fattest and fleeciest flocks, and their loyal hearts as offerings.

There were knights in armor on the roads that day, and soldiers in coats of mail, and lovely ladies. All had come to toast the King and his lovely Queen—and especially small Princess Aurora. The castle was gay with banners and flags and the courtyard was swarming with happy people. But the happiest of all were those in the throne room, close to the cradle of the royal child. They were good King Stefan and his Queen.

The King and Queen welcomed their royal guests—King Hubert of the neighboring kingdom and Prince Phillip, his small son. It had long been the dream of both friendly kings that one day their small kingdoms should be joined.

To do this Prince Phillip and little Princess Aurora would be betrothed. And when the princess came of age, the two of them would be wed.

Prince Phillip had brought a gift for the Princess. He felt quite grown-up when he presented it to the Queen.

Then he stepped to the cradle for a look at the small princess. Now babies did not interest Prince Phillip much. But at that moment his eye was caught by something that *did* interest him.

Three tiny, bright creatures floated down a beam of sunlight. They were the three good fairies—Mistress Flora, Mistress Fauna, and Mistress Merryweather. They too had come to present their gifts to the Princess.

Flora spoke first. "Little Princess," she said, "my gift shall be the gift of rare beauty." A shower of sunbeams shimmered down into the cradle.

Next Fauna said, "My gift is song your whole life long." Flower petals floated down upon the cradle.

Then Merryweather began, "Sweet Princess, my gift to you shall be—"

But before she could say any more, the wicked fairy Maleficent appeared.

"To show you that I bear no ill will for not being invited," Maleficent said, "I too shall bestow a gift on the child. Before the sun sets on her sixteenth birthday, the Princess shall prick her finger on the spindle of a spinning wheel—and die!"

"Oh, no!" gasped the Queen.

"Seize her!" cried the King.

But Maleficent disappeared in a bolt of lightning.

Then Merryweather spoke. "I cannot undo the curse, but I still have my wish. Sweet Princess, if you should prick your finger, you shall not die. You shall lie in a magic sleep and wake when true love's kiss shall break the spell."

"Burn every spinning wheel!" King Hubert said to King Stefan. "If there aren't any in the kingdom, the Princess can't prick her finger."

As night fell on Princess Aurora's christening day, the dusk was brightened with a fiery glow. In every town a great fire was kindled. And before those fires died, every spinning wheel in the kingdom had been burned.

In the deserted throne room the three fairies sat.

"Even a bonfire won't stop Maleficent," said Merryweather sadly.

"There must be some way," Flora muttered. "Walls may have ears," she said. "Follow me."

Flora swiftly turned herself into a tiny light and twinkled up to a jeweled box. The others followed her. Then they all settled down for a talk where even Maleficent couldn't overhear them.

"There's just one thing Maleficent won't expect," said Flora. "There's one thing she doesn't understand. And that is love."

Her voice dropped to an excited whisper. "Of course, we'll have to plan it carefully—Let's see, there's the woodcutter's cottage, the abandoned one. The King and Queen will object, but when we explain it's the only way—"

"Explain what?" asked Merryweather. "What are you talking about?"

"About the three peasant women raising a foundling child, deep in the forest."

"That's very nice of them," said Fauna. "Who are they?"

Flora waved her wand. Fauna and Merryweather looked at themselves in surprise. They were the peasant women!

"You mean," gasped Merryweather, "it's us?"

"Why not?" said Flora. "We'll take care of the baby."

"I'd like that!" said Merryweather. "And we'll have our magic, of course."

"No," said Flora sternly. "No magic!" And before they could protest, she snatched away their wands.

"You mean, live like mortals for sixteen years?" gasped Merryweather. "We've never done anything without magic. Who'll wash and cook and—?"

"Oh, we'll all pitch in," said Flora. "And that's why Maleficent won't suspect us."

"Well," said Merryweather and Fauna.

"Come," said Flora, "we must tell their majesties at once."

And off they went to the King and Queen, because it did indeed seem the best way to guard the baby princess from harm. The King and Queen agreed.

Good King Stefan and his beloved Queen watched with heavy hearts that night as the fairies and their daughter disappeared into the night.

clustered at a table, busy with a thick book of dress patterns.

"I pick this one," said Flora, putting her finger on a picture of a beautiful gown.

"Oh, she'll look beautiful in that," sighed Fauna.

"But how are we going to get her out of the house?" Merryweather, the practical one, said. "We can't surprise her if she's here."

Just then Briar Rose came down the stairs. They didn't see her until she spoke. "Well, what are you three dears up to?"

"Up to?" the aunts repeated.

"Why, my dear," said Merryweather hastily, "we want you to pick some berries."

"That's it," said the others, "lots of berries." And handing her a basket and her scarf, they all but pushed Briar Rose out the door.

So off into the woods went Briar Rose. And the aunts called after her:

"Don't hurry back!"

"But don't go too far!"

"And don't talk to strangers!"

"Good-bye, Good-bye, Good-bye!"

"I'll get the wands," said Merryweather, as soon as Briar Rose had gone.

"No wands," said Flora, "we're taking no chances."

"But I've never baked a cake," said poor Merryweather.

"You won't have to," said Fauna. "I'm going to bake the cake. I'm going to make it fifteen layers high, with pink and blue forget-me-nots, and candles."

"And I'm going to make the dress," said Flora.

Before Merryweather could ask a question, Flora flipped a length of cloth over her head. She slashed a hole at the bottom and a hole at the top, and holes in both sides, for sleeves.

"How does it look?" Flora asked her.

"It looks awful," said Merryweather crossly. "I still say we ought to use magic."

The years passed, as the years do, and for King Stefan and his Queen, they were lonely, anxious years.

But it was not so at the woodcutter's cottage, deep in the forest. Indeed, the little hut often rang with songs and merry laughter. For in that cottage the baby princess was growing into the loveliest of maidens . . . And what was her name? Well, the three aunts who had raised her with loving care called her Briar Rose.

At last it was almost the day of Briar Rose's birthday. What a flurry there was in the woodcutter's cottage! Briar Rose's three aunts, Flora, Fauna, and Merryweather, were

"But it's a lovely shade of pink," said Flora.

Merryweather said, "I wanted it blue."

Pink or blue, the dress did look awful. And it seemed likely that the cake would turn out worse.

Fauna tried to follow the recipe. But she didn't know that eggs had to be broken, and the layers of batter ran together in a mess.

"Enough of this nonsense," Merryweather snapped. "I'm going to get the wands."

And when she stamped up the stairs, with Flora's dress falling to pieces around her at each step, neither of the others could disagree.

While the fairies were having such a time at home, Briar Rose was spending a lonely day in the deep woods.

Because she had been protected all her life, the only friends Briar Rose had were the woodland animals and birds. As soon as she sat down on a fallen tree trunk, they surrounded her. The sleepy rabbits woke up from their naps and the saucy squirrels came running.

But today it was a bit sad. Suddenly the woodland friends were not quite enough any more.

"Oh dear!" Briar Rose said. "Why do they still treat me like a child?"

"Whooo?" asked the owl.

"Aunt Flora and Fauna and Merryweather," said Briar Rose. "And I so much want to meet someone."

"Whooo?" asked the owl.

"Oh," said Briar Rose, "someone tall and handsome and romantic. We'd walk together and talk together—well, it's only a dream." And because it was only a dream, Briar Rose sadly hid her face in her hands.

Now it happened that on that very day the Prince of the neighboring country, Phillip by name, was riding alone through the woods. Suddenly he stopped, for he thought he heard a beautiful song.

It was Briar Rose he heard. She could not stay sad for long and was singing.

"Do you hear that, Samson?" Phillip said to his horse. "Come on, let's find out who it is."

As the Prince came up behind Briar Rose on the woodland path, he thought she was the loveliest thing he had ever seen.

"I know you," Briar Rose sang to Phillip. "I walked with you once upon a dream."

"I know you," the Prince sang with her. He caught Briar Rose in his arms and they danced down the path.

"Oh!" said Briar Rose, pulling free. "I forgot, you're a—a—"

"A stranger?" asked the Prince.

"Yes," said Briar Rose.

"But we've met before. Don't you remember? You said so yourself," the Prince said, "once upon a dream."

"Oh!" said Briar Rose, and she let the Prince take her hand in his. Together they walked down the woodland path singing their song.

"Who are you?" the Prince asked. "What is your name?"

"My name is—oh, no, I mustn't," cried Briar Rose, remembering her aunts' warnings. "Good-bye!"

And away she ran, toward home.

"When will I see you?" the Prince called.

"Never, oh, never, never!" Briar Rose called back sadly.

"When?" the Prince asked again. "Tomorrow?"

He seemed terribly sad, and that was too much for Briar Rose to bear. She wanted him to be happy.

"Not tomorrow," Briar Rose said, because suddenly it seemed so far away. "This evening—at the woodcutter's cottage in the woods."

Back at the cottage, preparations for the surprise party were going on more smoothly, with the help of the fairies' magic wands.

Flour, eggs and milk mixed together and made a lovely cake. Needle flashed up and down and sewed a beautiful ball gown.

As he flew over the cottage, his sharp eyes saw something—a magic cloud of pink. Then out came another magic cloud—but this one was blue! Sput—pink! Sput—blue! Pink! Blue! Pink! Blue!

Down came the raven and alighted on the chimney's edge. He leaned forward and— Sput! A cloud of pink magic hit him in the face!

Away Maleficent's raven flew, bright pink, just as Briar Rose came singing down the path. He had seen magic in the woods and that was enough.

"Not pink!" cried Merryweather, as she stepped back to look at the dress, which had been made by magic. "Oh, no! Let's make it blue!" And with a flash of her wand, she changed the color of the dress.

"Pink!" cried Flora, changing it back.

"Blue!" cried Merryweather. And so it went. The fairies did not realize that puffs of pink and blue magic were spouting from the chimney with each flash of their wands.

It happened that a raven was flying over the forest, and this raven was Maleficent's pet bird. He had been sent out to find the Princess before the sixteen-year curse ran out. And this was the very last day. He shivered uneasily thinking of what Maleficent would do to him if he did not succeed in his task.

"Once upon a dream," Briar Rose was singing as she opened the cottage door. "Aunt Flora," she called, eager to share her happy news. "Fauna! Merryweather! Where is everybody?"

Then she saw the new dress draped on a chair. And she saw the magic layer cake on the table.

"Oh! How lovely!" Briar Rose said.

"Surprise!" cried the fairies, popping out from their hiding places. "Happy birthday!"

"Oh, you darlings," said Briar Rose. "This is the happiest day of my life. Everything is so wonderful. Just wait till you meet him."

"Him?" gasped the fairies. "You've met some stranger?"

"Oh, he's not a stranger," Briar Rose said. "We've met before."

"Where?" asked the fairies.

"Once upon a dream," sighed Briar Rose, closing her eyes.

"She's in love!" cried Fauna.

"Oh, no!" cried Merryweather.

"This is terrible," wailed Flora.

"But why?" asked Briar Rose. "After all, I am sixteen."

"But you're already betrothed," Flora explained sadly. "You have been since the day you were born, to Prince Phillip."

"That's impossible," said Briar Rose. "To marry a Prince, I'd have to be a—"

"Princess," broke in Merryweather. "And you are, dear. You are Princess Aurora. And tonight we are taking you home to your father, King Stefan."

"I can't go," said Briar Rose. "He's coming here tonight. I asked him to call."

"I'm sorry, child," said Fauna kindly. "But you must never see your young man again."

"Oh, no, no!" sobbed Briar Rose, bursting into tears. And she stumbled up the stairs to her room.

Behind her the three fairies stood staring unhappily at the cake and dress.

"And we thought she'd be so pleased," Merryweather sighed.

The golden light of the late afternoon warmed the ancient castle walls as the three fairies hurried an unhappy Briar Rose up side roads and byways to her rightful home.

Shadows were deepening around them as they slipped into the courtyard by a small door. Unseen and silent, they quickly crossed the courtyard and disappeared through a shadowy archway into the castle itself. Then down dim halls and up circular stairs they went. And at last Flora, who was leading them, opened the door to the Princess's own room.

"All right, dear," Flora whispered. "In here." And in they went, very quietly and all on tiptoe.

"Bolt the doors, Merryweather," Flora ordered. "Fauna, pull the drapes. Until the evening sun has set, we are not safe from Maleficent or the curse." Flora's bright gaze darted to every side. Not a sign of danger did she see.

"Sit down, dear," said Flora, "and make yourself at home while we go to see your father to find out if—if there is anything more we can do."

What the loving fairies hoped was that they could find a way to make the Princess's dream of seeing her young man again come true. So off they fluttered, leaving Briar Rose —or Princess Aurora, as she was called in the castle—sobbing in the dim and lonely dusk.

The very day her dream of a wonderful stranger came to life, the day of her birthday, was turning out to be the unhappiest day of the Princess's life.

Meanwhile the castle of King Stefan was all a-bustle. There was not a person in the country who did not know that today was the day Princess Aurora was coming home.

The news had traveled far beyond the country's borders. King Hubert of the neighboring kingdom had already arrived at the castle. For, as everyone knew, at the birthday ball the wedding of the young Princess Aurora and her Prince would be announced.

In the royal study, King Stefan and King Hubert were busy with plans.

"And we've already built a cottage," Hubert said. "The lovebirds can move in tomorrow. Nothing elaborate, of course. Just forty bedrooms, ten dining halls, and—"

"But Hubert," said Stefan sadly, "I haven't even seen my daughter yet. And you're taking her away from me!"

They were interrupted by a herald's shout: "His Royal Highness, Prince Phillip!"

"My son!" cried Hubert. He raced to greet the Prince.

"Hurry, son," Hubert said. "Change into something suitable. You can't meet your future bride looking like that."

"But I have met her, father," said Phillip.

King Hubert was almost speechless with surprise. "You have?" he gasped. "But where?"

"Oh, once upon a dream," sang Phillip.

"Stop all this nonsense about dreams," snapped his father.

"But it wasn't only a dream, father," said Phillip more seriously. "I really did meet her."

"The Princess Aurora?" said his father. "Good heavens, we must tell Stefan."

"I didn't say it was Aurora," Phillip reminded him. "I said I met the girl I am going to marry. I don't know who she was—a peasant girl, I suppose."

"A peasant girl!" cried King Hubert. "You're going to marry—Oh, Phillip, you're joking, of course."

But Prince Phillip was not joking.

"You can't do this to me!" his father said. "You're a prince and you're going to marry a princess! I won't have it!"

"Now, father," said Phillip, "you're living in the past. This is the fourteenth century. And I am going to marry the girl I love, even if it means giving up the throne."

"Nonsense!" said King Hubert.

"Very well," said Phillip. And with a shrug of his shoulders, he swung himself up into Samson's saddle and turned away.

"Phillip!" said his father. "Come back, son!"

But Phillip was out of the castle gates and off on the road to the woods.

Behind him King Hubert sank down on the steps, holding his head in his hands. "How will I ever tell Stefan," he moaned.

But worse was still to come.

Unaware of all that was going on, Aurora still sobbed in her room. Then a thread of melody drifted into the room and made her feel warm and soothed.

The melody beckoned. As if in a spell, Aurora followed it. The fireplace opened and she mounted the stairs behind it.

Even the fairies heard the music. But by the time they raced back into the room, Aurora had already disappeared up the magic stairs. They were too late.

Meanwhile, the Princess, still under a spell, moved toward the shadows where Maleficent stood near a spinning wheel.

"Don't touch anything!" the fairies called.

But Maleficent's evil voice rang out:

"Touch the spindle!"

Aurora sleepily stretched out her hand.

Prick! The spindle scratched her skin. Aurora crumpled to the floor.

"You poor simple fools," Maleficent sneered at the fairies, "thinking that your puny powers could defeat me." And with an evil laugh, Maleficent vanished in a puff of black smoke.

"Poor King Stefan," sighed Fauna. "And the Queen. They'll be heartbroken when they find out."

"They're not going to find out," said Flora. "We'll put them all to sleep until the Princess awakens."

Off the fairies flew through the castle, scattering their magic stardust, until everyone in the castle was wrapped in a blanket of magic, peaceful sleep.

Just as the fairies left the castle, Prince Phillip was coming to the tiny cottage in the woods.

But it was not the girl he loved who waited behind the curtains. It was Maleficent.

Outside Phillip squared his shoulders, straightened his cloak, and knocked at the cottage door.

"Come in," called Maleficent sweetly.

Phillip swung the door open and stepped inside.

And before Phillip, blinking at the darkness, could tell what was happening, Maleficent cried out, "Away with him!"

And from the darkness on every side evil spirits came swooping. Soon Phillip and Samson were helplessly caught in their nets. Then away the evil spirits flew, bearing their captives to the dismal dungeons of Maleficent's castle of darkness.

Soon after, but too late, the three fairies pushed open the door. They knew immediately that something was wrong.

"Maleficent!" they cried out together, when they saw the prince's hat. And without a thought for their own safety, they flew off through the woods towards the castle of Maleficent.

196

Meanwhile, Maleficent taunted Phillip, her great black cape billowing about her.

"Think," Maleficent said, "that in the top-most tower of King Stefan's castle the Princess Aurora sleeps—and she is the selfsame peasant maid who won your heart just yesterday in the forest glade."

Phillip looked up in surprise. The Princess Aurora his own true love? And here he was a prisoner!

"She is indeed most wondrous fair," Maleficent's cruel voice went on. "And she will sleep through the ages, lacking this—the magic of her true love's kiss!"

Her true love's kiss! Phillip sprang to his feet. He must go to her! But his chains held him back.

Phillip held his head in his hands while Maleficent laughed.

"Come, my pet," Maleficent whispered to her pet raven, "let us leave our noble prince with his thoughts."

Soon the dungeon door clanked shut behind them. Phillip and Samson were left alone in the dark.

At last the good fairies reached the castle of evil. Down they flew into the deep dungeon.

"How did you get here?" Phillip asked.

"Shh!" said Flora. "No time to explain."

Sparks shot out from the three tiny wands and the Prince's chains fell off.

"Now," said Flora, "be on your way armed with this enchanted shield of virtue and this mighty sword of truth. For these are the weapons of good that will win over evil."

Phillip sprang to Samson's back and away he galloped.

Hearing him, Maleficent screamed with rage, "Up with the drawbridge!"

On raced Samson. Up swung the bridge. A deep chasm lay below. The horse gathered himself for a mighty leap and carried Phillip safely to the farther side.

As Prince Phillip vanished from her sight, Maleficent's face twisted with anger. She cried into the darkness:

"Poison thorn and witch's knell
Round Stefan's castle cast my spell!"

The good fairies, flying at the prince's side, were the first to see the terrible hedge of thorns.

"The sword of truth!" they called out. "Its power will cut through the hedge."

Slash! Slash! Phillip swung the sword this

way and that. Soon he cleared a hole in the hedge just big enough for Samson to leap through.

"The castle at last!" Phillip said.

But Maleficent had not given up. And before Phillip's eyes, a huge fire-breathing dragon reared its head.

It flung Phillip from Samson's saddle. Down fell the sword of truth and the shield of virtue.

But the good fairies swooped up the shield and slipped it over Phillip's arm, and they slid the sword of truth to within his reach.

"Swish!" came the dragon's fiery breath. But the shield of virtue turned back the flames. Slash! came the dragon's sharp teeth. But the Prince struck with his sword.

The dreadful dragon of evil lay slain. And the Prince led Samson up to the gate of the great castle.

With the help of the good fairies, Prince

Phillip found his way through the castle, right to the room where Aurora lay asleep.

For a moment the prince stood staring. She was even more lovely than he had remembered. Then, kneeling, he bent over her. Princess Aurora awakened at the touch of love's first kiss.

All through the sleeping castle went a sigh. The torch bearers awoke and stretched. In the courtyard the fountain awoke with a flutter of tinkling drops. In the kitchens the cooks all rubbed their eyes and dipped their spoons into bubbling pots again.

And in the throne room, King Hubert, King Stefan, and King Stefan's Queen were dozing side by side.

Stefan awoke first. "Forgive me, Hubert!" he said to his guest, "You were saying—?"

"Er—uh," yawned Hubert rousing slowly. "I was?" Then he remembered his scene with Prince Phillip. It seemed so long ago! But he still had to face his bitter task. He still had to tell Stefan that his son Phillip refused to marry Stefan's daughter Aurora.

"Oh, yes," Hubert began vaguely. "After all, Stefan, this is the fourteenth century."

"You said that," said Stefan, "a moment ago."

"Well, what I mean is," said Hubert. "Oh, dash it, to come right to the point, my son Phillip says he's going to marry—"

A blare of trumpets interrupted him, and

the voice of the royal herald rang through the hall.

"Their royal highness, Princess Aurora and Prince Phillip!"

And, to the music of the royal orchestra, Princess Aurora made her first appearance on the arm of her true love, the handsome young Prince.

King Stefan and his Queen watched wide-eyed as their lovely daughter came toward them down the grand staircase.

"It's Aurora!" said Stefan. His hand was trembling. "She's here!"

Hubert turned to look. He rubbed his eyes. Then he smiled proudly. The young man was Phillip.

Meanwhile, from a balcony high above, the three good fairies looked down happily.

Their beloved Briar Rose, now Princess Aurora, was reunited with her parents after sixteen long years.

There were tears of joy in King Hubert's eyes as he watched the happy scene. But when he turned to his tall young son, he tried to make his voice sound stern.

"What does this mean?" Hubert asked. "I simply don't understand."

"It's the happy ending, father," Prince Phillip explained. "The happy ending to a story that started once upon a dream."

Then Prince Phillip caught the Princess by the hand. To the swelling music of the royal orchestra, they waltzed into the land of their dreams. There they lived happily ever after, you may be sure.

High above them the fairies watched. Fauna dabbed at her eyes.

"What is the matter, dear?" her sister Flora asked.

"Oh," sniffed Fauna. "I love happy endings." And her tears fell.

"Yes," sighed Flora, wiping her own eyes, "so do I."

But, just then, Flora's eye fell on the Princess's gown.

"Oh dear! Blue!" she said. And at the flash of her magic wand, the gown turned to pink.

Merryweather had been watching the dancing. But as the gown turned pink, she gasped. Up came her wand.

"Blue!" she whispered.

And that was how it happened that, as she danced, the Princess's gown kept flashing from blue to pink to blue, right up to

THE END

BAMBI

BAMBI came into the world in the middle of a forest thicket. The little, hidden thicket was scarcely big enough for the new baby and his mother.

But the magpie soon spied him there.

"What a beautiful baby!" she cried. And away she flew to spread the news to all the other animals of the forest.

Her chattering soon brought dozens of birds and animals to the thicket. The rabbits came hurrying; the squirrels came a-scurrying. The robins and bluebirds fluttered and flew.

At last even the old owl woke up from his long day's sleep.

"Who, who?" the owl said sleepily, hearing all the commotion.

"Wake up, Friend Owl!" a rabbit called. "It's happened! The young Prince is born!"

"Everyone's going to see him," said the squirrels. "You come, too."

With a sigh the owl spread his wings and flew off toward the thicket. There he found squirrels and rabbits and birds peering through the bushes at a doe and a little spotted fawn.

The fawn was Bambi, the new Prince of the Forest.

"Congratulations," said the owl, speaking for all the animals. "This is quite an occasion. It isn't often that a Prince is born in the forest."

The doe looked up. "Thank you," she said quietly. Then with her nose she gently nudged her sleeping baby until he lifted his head and looked around.

She nudged him again, and licked him reassuringly. At last he pushed up on his thin legs, trying to stand.

"Look! He's trying to stand up already!" shouted one of the little rabbits, Thumper by name. "He's wobbly, though, isn't he?"

"Thumper!" the mother rabbit exclaimed, "that's not a pleasant thing to say!"

The new fawn's legs were not very steady, it was true, but at last he stood ,beside his mother. Now all the animals could see the fine white spots on his red-brown coat, and the sleepy expression on his soft baby face.

The forest around him echoed with countless small voices. A soft breeze rustled the leaves about the thicket. And the watching animals whispered among themselves. But the little fawn did not listen to any of them. He only knew that his mother's tongue was licking him softly, washing and warming him. He nestled closer to her, and closed his eyes.

Quietly the animals and birds slipped away through the forest.

Thumper the rabbit was the last to go.

"What are you going to name the young Prince?" he asked.

"I'll call him Bambi," the mother answered.

"Bambi," Thumper repeated. "Bambi. That's a good name. Good-bye, Bambi." And he hopped away after his sisters.

Bambi was not a sleepy baby for long. Soon he was following his mother down the narrow forest paths. Bright flowers winked from beneath the leaves.

Squirrels and chipmunks looked up and called, "Good morning, young Prince."

Opossums, hanging by their long tails from a tree branch, said, "Hello, Prince Bambi."

The fawn looked at them all with wondering eyes. But he did not say a word.

Finally, as Bambi and his mother reached a little clearing in the forest, they met Thumper and his family.

"Hi, Bambi," said Thumper. "Let's play."

"Yes, let's play," Thumper's sister cried. And away they hopped, over branches and hillocks and tufts of grass.

Bambi soon understood the game, and he began to jump and run on his stiff, spindly legs.

Thumper jumped over a log and his sisters followed.

"Come on, Bambi," Thumper called. "Hop over the log."

Bambi jumped, but not far enough. He fell with a plop on top of the log.

"Too bad," said Thumper. "You'll do better next time."

Bambi untangled his legs and stood up again. But still he did not speak. He pranced along behind Thumper, and soon he saw a family of birds sitting on a branch.

Bambi looked at them.

"Those are birds, Bambi," Thumper told him. "Birds."

"Bir-d," Bambi said slowly. The young Prince had spoken his first word!

Thumper and his sisters were all excited, and Bambi himself was pleased. He repeated the word over and over to himself. Then he saw a butterfly cross the path. "Bird, bird!" he cried again.

"No, Bambi," said Thumper. "That's not a bird. That's a butterfly."

The butterfly disappeared into a clump of yellow flowers. Bambi bounded toward them happily.

"Butterfly!" he cried.

"No, Bambi," said Thumper. "Not butterfly. *Flower.*"

He pushed his nose into the flowers and sniffed. Bambi did the same, but suddenly he drew back. His nose had touched something warm and furry.

Out from the bed of flowers came a small black head with two shining eyes.

"Flower!" said Bambi.

The black eyes twinkled. As the little animal stepped out, the white stripe down his black furry back glistened in the sun.

Thumper the rabbit was laughing so hard that he could scarcely speak.

"That's not a flower," said Thumper. "That's a skunk."

"Flower," repeated Bambi.

"I don't care," said the skunk. "The young Prince can call me Flower if he wants to. I don't mind."

So Flower, the skunk, got his name.

One morning Bambi and his mother walked down a new path. It grew lighter and lighter as they walked along. Soon the trail ended in a tangle of bushes and vines, and Bambi could see a great, bright, open space spread out before them.

Bambi wanted to bound out there to play in the sunshine, but his mother stopped him. "Wait," she said. "You must never run out on the meadow without making sure it is safe."

She took a few slow, careful steps forward. She listened and sniffed in all directions. Then she called, "Come."

Bambi bounded out. He felt so good and so happy that he leaped into the air again and again. For the meadow was the most beautiful place he had ever seen.

His mother dashed forward and showed him how to race and play in the tall grass.

Bambi ran after her. He felt as if he were flying. Round and round they raced in great circles. At last his mother stopped and stood still, catching her breath.

Then Bambi set out by himself to explore the meadow. Soon he spied his little friend the skunk, sitting in the shade of some blossoms.

"Good morning, Flower," said Bambi.

And he found Thumper and his sisters nibbling sweet clover.

"Try some, Bambi," said Thumper.

So Bambi did.

Suddenly a big green frog popped out of the clover patch and hopped over to a meadow pond. Bambi had not seen the pond before, so he hurried over for a closer look.

As the fawn came near, the frog hopped into the water.

Where could he have gone? Bambi wondered. So he bent down to look into the pond. As the ripples cleared, Bambi jumped back. For he saw a fawn down there in the water, looking out at him!

"Don't be frightened, Bambi," his mother told him. "You are just seeing yourself in the water."

NEY G.S. BK—O

So Bambi looked once more. This time he saw *two* fawns looking back at him! He jumped back again, and as he lifted his head he saw that it was true—there was another little fawn standing beside him!

"Hello," she said.

Bambi backed away and ran to his mother, where she was quietly eating grass beside another doe. Bambi leaned against her and peered out at the other little fawn, who had followed him.

"Don't be afraid, Bambi," his mother said. "This is little Faline, and this is your Aunt Ena. Can't you say hello to them?"

"Hello, Bambi," said the two deer. But Bambi did not say a word.

"You have been wanting to meet other deer," his mother reminded him. "Well, Aunt Ena and Faline are deer like us. Now can't you speak to them?"

"Hello," whispered Bambi in a small, small voice.

"Come and play, Bambi," said Faline. She leaned forward and licked his face.

Bambi dashed away as fast as he could run, and Faline raced after him. They almost flew over that meadow.

Up and down they chased each other. Over the little hillocks they raced.

When they stopped, all topsy-turvy and breathless, they were good friends.

Then they walked side by side on the bright meadow, visiting quietly together.

One morning, Bambi woke up shivering with cold. Even before he opened his eyes, his nose told him there was something new and strange in the world. Then he looked out of the thicket. Everything was covered with white.

"It is snow, Bambi," his mother said. "Go ahead and walk out. It is all right."

Bambi stepped out onto the snow very cautiously. His feet sank deep into the soft blanket. He had to lift them up high as he walked along. Now and then, with a soft plop, a tiny snowy heap would tumble from a leaf overhead onto his nose or back.

Bambi was delighted. The sun glittered so brightly on the whiteness. The air was so mild and clear. And all around him white snow stars came whirling down.

From the crest of a little hill he saw Thumper. Thumper was sitting on the top of the pond!

"Come on, Bambi!" Thumper shouted. "Look! The water's stiff!" He thumped with one foot against the solid ice. "You can even slide on it. Watch and I'll show you how!"

Thumper took a run and slid swiftly across the pond. Bambi tried it, too, but his legs shot out from under him and down he crashed on the hard ice. That was not so much fun.

"Let's play something else," Bambi suggested, when he had carefully pulled himself to his feet again. "Where's Flower?"

"I think I know," said Thumper.

He led Bambi to the doorway of a deep burrow. They peered down into it. There, peacefully sleeping on a bed of withered flowers, lay the little skunk.

"Wake up, Flower!" Bambi called.

"Is it spring yet?" Flower asked sleepily, half opening his eyes.

"No, winter's just beginning," Bambi said. "What are you doing?"

"Hibernating," the little skunk replied. "Flowers always sleep in the winter, you know."

Thumper yawned. "I guess I'll take a nap, too," he said. "Good-bye, Bambi. I'll see you later."

So Bambi wandered back to the thicket.

"Don't fret, Bambi," his mother said. "Winter will soon be over, and spring will come again."

So Bambi went to sleep beside his mother in the snug, warm thicket, and dreamed of the jolly games that he and his friends would play in the wonderful spring to come.

PINOCCHIO

ONE NIGHT, long, long ago, the Evening Star shone down across the dark sky. Its beams formed a shimmering pathway to a tiny village, and painted its humble roofs with stardust.

But the silent little town was deep in sleep. The only witness to the beauty of the night was a weary wayfarer who chanced to be passing through.

His clothes were gray with dust. His well-worn shoes pinched his feet; his back ached from the weight of the carpetbag slung over his shabby shoulder. To be sure, it was only a small carpetbag; but this wayfarer had a very small shoulder. As a matter of fact, he was an exceedingly small wayfarer. His name was Cricket, Jiminy Cricket.

He marveled at the radiant star; it seemed almost close enough to touch, and pretty as a picture. But at this moment Jiminy Cricket was not interested in pretty pictures. He was looking for a place to rest.

Suddenly he noticed a light in a window, and smoke curling from a chimney.

"Where there's smoke, there's a fire," he reasoned. "Where there's a fire, there's a hearth. And where there's a hearth, there *should* be a cricket!"

And with that, he hopped up to the window sill and peered in. The room had a friendly look. So Jiminy crawled under the door, scurried over to the hearth, backed up against the glowing fireplace, and warmed his little britches.

It was no ordinary village home into which the small wayfarer had stumbled. It was a workshop: the workshop of Geppetto the woodcarver. Old Geppetto was working late that night. He was making a puppet.

Geppetto lived alone except for his black kitten, Figaro, and a pet goldfish he called Cleo. But he had many friends; everyone knew and loved the kindly, white-haired old man. He had spent his whole life creating happiness for others.

It was the children who loved Geppetto best. He doctored their dolls, put clean sawdust into limp rag bodies and painted fresh smiles on faded china faces. He fashioned new arms and legs for battered tin soldiers—and there was magic in his hands when he carved a toy.

Now, the weary old fellow put his tools away and surveyed his newest handiwork. The puppet he had made had the figure of a small boy. He was the right size for a small boy. He had the cute, round face of a small boy—except for one feature. The nose! Geppetto had given him a very long and pointed nose, such a nose as no real boy ever possessed. A funny nose.

The old woodcarver stroked his chin and chuckled. "Woodenhead," he said, "you are finished, and you deserve a name. What shall I call you? I know—*Pinocchio!* Do you like it?" He worked the puppet's strings so that it nodded "Yes."

"That settles it!" cried Geppetto happily. "Pinocchio you are! And now," he yawned, "time for bed. Good night, Figaro! Good night, Cleo! Good night, Pinocchio!"

Jiminy Cricket was glad to hear these words, for he felt very sleepy. Geppetto put on a long white nightshirt and climbed creakily into bed, but he still sat admiring the puppet with its wooden smile.

"Look at him, Figaro!" he exclaimed. "He seems almost real. Wouldn't it be nice if he were alive?"

But the only answer from the kitten was a snore.

Long after Geppetto had gone to sleep, Jiminy Cricket lay awake thinking. It made him sad to realize the old man's wish could never come true.

Suddenly he heard something. Music—mysterious music! He sat up and looked around the room. Then he saw a strange light—a brilliant glow, which grew more dazzling every minute. It was a star—the Evening Star, floating down the sky and entering Geppetto's window!

Then in the center of its blinding glow appeared a beautiful lady dressed in robes of flowing blue.

"As I live and breathe!" Jiminy whispered in astonishment. "A fairy!"

The Blue Fairy bent over the old woodcarver and spoke to him ever so softly, so as not to disturb his slumber.

"Good Geppetto," she said, "you have given so much happiness to others, you deserve to have your wish come true!"

Then she turned to the wooden puppet. Holding out her glittering wand, she spoke these words:

> *Little puppet made of pine,*
> *Wake! The gift of life is thine!*

And when the wand touched him, Pinocchio came to life! First he blinked his eyes, then he raised his wooden arm and wiggled his jointed fingers.

"I can move!" he cried. "I can *talk*!"

"Yes, Pinocchio," the Blue Fairy smiled. "Geppetto needs a little son. So tonight I give you life."

"Then I'm a real boy!" cried Pinocchio.

"No," said the Fairy sadly. "There is no magic that can make us real. I have given you life—the rest is up to you."

"Tell me what I must do," begged Pinocchio. "I want to be a real boy!"

"Prove yourself brave, truthful, and un-selfish," said the Blue Fairy. "Be a good son to Geppetto—make him proud of you! Then, some day, you will wake up and find yourself a real boy!"

"Whew! That won't be easy," thought Jiminy Cricket.

But the Blue Fairy also realized what a hard task she was giving Pinocchio. "The world is full of temptations," she continued. "You must learn to choose between right and wrong—"

"Right? Wrong?" questioned Pinocchio. "How will I know?"

Jiminy wrung his hands in desperation. But the wise Fairy was not yet finished. "Your conscience will tell you the difference between right and wrong," she explained.

"What is conscience?" Pinocchio asked.

That was too much for Jiminy Cricket. He hopped down where he could be seen.

"A conscience," he shouted, "is that still small voice people won't listen to! That's the trouble with the world today!"

"Are *you* my conscience?" asked Pinocchio eagerly.

Jiminy was embarrassed, but the Blue Fairy came to his rescue. "Would you like to be Pinocchio's conscience?" she smiled. "You seem a man of the world. What is your name?"

Jiminy was flattered. "Jiminy Cricket," he answered.

"Kneel, Mister Cricket," commanded the Blue Fairy and Jiminy knelt.

"I dub you Pinocchio's conscience," she proclaimed, "Lord High Keeper of the Knowledge of Right and Wrong! Arise—*Sir* Jiminy Cricket!"

And when the dusty little cricket rose his shabby old clothes were gone and he was clad in elegant raiment from head to foot.

"Don't I get a badge or something?" he asked.

"We'll see," the Blue Fairy smiled.

"Make it a gold one?" urged Jiminy.

"Perhaps, if you do your job well," she said. "I leave Pinocchio in your hands. Give him the benefit of your advice and experience. Help him to be a real boy!"

It was a serious moment for the little cricket. He promised to help Pinocchio as much as he could, and to stick by him through thick and thin. The Blue Fairy thanked him.

"And now, Pinocchio," she said, "be a good boy—and always let your conscience be your guide! Don't be discouraged because you are different from the other boys! Remember—*any child who is not good, might just as well be made of wood!*" The Blue Fairy backed slowly away. There was one last soft chord of music and she was gone.

Pinocchio and Jiminy stared silently at the spot where the Fairy had stood, half hoping she might return. The little cricket finally broke the spell.

"Say, she's all right, son!" he exclaimed. "Remember what she told you—always let your conscience be your guide!"

"Yes sir, I will!" answered Pinocchio.

"And when you need me, whistle," said Jiminy, "like this!"

"Like this?" Pinocchio tried, but no sound came.

So Jiminy sang him a little lecture-lesson, which went something like this:

> *"When you get in trouble*
> *And you don't know*
> *right from wrong,*
> *Give a little whistle,*
> *Give a little whistle.*
> *When you meet temptation*
> *And the urge is very strong,*
> *Give a little whistle,*
> *Give a little whistle.*

Then he began dancing down the strings of a violin on the bench, balancing himself with his small umbrella.

> *"Take the straight and narrow path*
> *And if you start to slide,*
> *Give a little whistle,*
> *Give a little whistle—"*

Just then the violin string broke. Jiminy fell over backward, but picked himself up and finished, "and always let your conscience be your guide!"

Pinocchio watched entranced as the little cricket went on dancing. Finally he too jumped up and tried to make his wooden feet go through the same steps. But he danced too close to the edge of the workbench, lost his balance and fell clatteringly to the floor.

The noise woke Geppetto. "Who's there?" he called.

Pinocchio, on the floor, answered, "It's *me!*"

Geppetto's teeth chattered with fright. "Figaro, there's somebody in here!" he whispered. "A burglar, maybe! Come, we'll catch him!"

Then to his surprise, he noticed his puppet, which he had left on the workbench, lying on the floor.

"Why, Pinocchio!" he exclaimed. "How did you get down there?" He picked the puppet up and set him back on the bench. Imagine his surprise when Pinocchio answered!

"I fell down!" he said.

Geppetto stared. "What! You're talking?" he cried. "No! You're only a marionette. You can't talk!"

"Yes, I can," insisted the puppet. "I can move, too!"

The old man backed away. "No, no," he argued. "I must be dreaming! I will pour water on myself! I will stick me with pins!"

Geppetto made sure he was awake. "Now we will see who is dreaming," he challenged. "Go on—say something!"

Pinocchio laughed merrily. "Do it again!" he begged. "You're very funny! I like you!"

"You *do* talk," said the old man, in a hushed voice. "Pinocchio! It's a miracle! Figaro! Cleo! Look—he's alive!"

Geppetto didn't know whether to laugh or cry, he was so happy. "This calls for a celebration!" he announced. He turned on a music box and began to dance. He went to his toy shelves and filled his arms with playthings. It was just like Christmas for Pinocchio. He couldn't decide which toy to play with first.

But the music box ran down and the celebration ended.

"Now it is time for bed," said the old woodcarver. "Come, Pinocchio. You shall sleep here in this dresser drawer." He tucked Pinocchio in and said, "Sleep fast, Pinocchio!"

That night Jiminy Cricket did an unusual thing—for him. He prayed. He prayed that Pinocchio might never disappoint that kind, happy old man or the lovely Blue Fairy, and that he himself might be a good conscience, so Pinocchio would soon earn the right to be a real boy.

All was still in the little shop. High in the sky the Evening Star twinkled softly, as though smiling approval of a good night's work.

Morning dawned bright and clear. As the school bells rang out over the village, their clamor sent pigeons flying from the old belfry like colored fans spread against the white clouds.

The school bells carried a special message of joy to old Geppetto. Today his own son was to join the other little ones on their way to school!

Pinocchio too was impatient. His face, shiny from scrubbing, beamed with excitement. Even Figaro and Cleo realized it was a gala day.

At last Pinocchio was pronounced ready. Geppetto opened the door. For the first time the puppet looked out at the wide, wide world. How beautiful it was!

"What are those?" he asked, pointing down the street.

"Those are the children, bless them!" Geppetto answered. "They are the boys and girls —your schoolmates, Pinocchio!"

"Real boys?" Pinocchio asked eagerly.

"Yes, my son. And if you study hard, you'll soon be as smart as they are. Wait a minute—your books!"

Little Figaro appeared at the door, tugging the strap which held Pinocchio's schoolbooks.

"Ah, thank you, Figaro. You too want to help! Pinocchio, here are your books. Remember, be a good boy. Choose your friends carefully; shun evil companions. Mind the teacher—"

"Good-bye!" shouted Pinocchio, pulling carelessly away. But he thought better of it, ran back and threw his arms around Geppetto. "Good-bye, Father," he said shyly; then off he marched, his books under his arm, chock-full of good resolutions.

Jiminy Cricket heard the school bell and jumped up in a great hurry. Suppose Pinocchio had gone off to school without him! If ever a small boy needs a conscience, it is on his first day at school. A fine time to oversleep, Jiminy thought. Then he stuffed

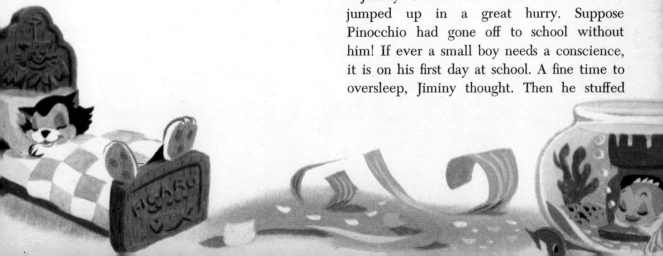

his shirt hastily inside his trousers, grabbed his hat and rushed out.

"Hey, Pinoke!" he called. "Wait for me!"

"An extra mouth to feed, Figaro," Geppetto chuckled cheerfully to the kitten. "Yet what a joy it is to have someone to work for!"

But alas, many a dreary day and night were to pass before the old woodcarver saw his boy again! For in spite of Geppetto's warning, Pinocchio fell into bad company. He met two scheming adventurers—a Fox and a Cat, the worst pair of scoundrels in the whole countryside.

Run down at the heel and patched at the seat, these villains managed somehow to look like elegant gentlemen out for a stroll. But as usual, they were up to no good.

Suddenly, "Look!" cried the sharp-eyed Fox, who went by the name of J. Worthington Foulfellow, alias Honest John. "Do you see what I see?" He pointed with his cane. The stupid Cat, who was called Gideon, stared at Pinocchio.

"A puppet that walks!" marveled Foulfellow. "A live puppet—a marionette without strings! A breathing woodenhead!"

And before Pinocchio knew what had happened, he was lying flat on his face. Something had tripped him up, and that something was a cane, thrust between his feet by the sly old fox.

"My dear young man! I'm so sorry," Foulfellow apologized, helping Pinocchio to his feet. "A most regrettable accident—Mr.—er—"

"Pinocchio," answered the little puppet cheerfully.

"Ha ha, Pinocchio," began Foulfellow, "you were going a little too fast! A little too fast, and in the *wrong* direction. Now I have a plan for you. Come . . ."

"But I'm on my way to school," said Pinocchio.

"To school? Nonsense!" said Foulfellow. "I have a much better plan."

"You're too bright a boy to waste your time in school," said Foulfellow. "Isn't he, Gideon?" Gideon nodded.

"You deserve a trip to Pleasure Island, my boy," said sly old Foulfellow.

"Pleasure Island?" repeated Pinocchio.

"Pleasure Island!" cried Foulfellow. "Where every day is a holiday, with fireworks, brass bands, parades—a paradise for boys! Why, I can see you now—lolling under a doughnut tree, a lollipop in each hand, gazing off at the pink Ice Cream Mountains —think of it, Pinocchio!"

It was a tempting picture the sly fox painted. "Well, I *was* going to school," said Pinocchio. He hesitated. "But perhaps I could go to Pleasure Island first—for a little while . . ."

"Oh, what a woodenhead he is!" thought Jiminy Cricket, panting along behind. He was too late to stop the three of them strolling off together.

So he loyally followed.

Soon they came to a great coach, piled to the brim with boys—eager, noisy, impudent boys! Laughing and shouting, Pinocchio climbed aboard.

"Good-bye!" Pinocchio called to the Fox. "I'll never be able to thank you for this!"

"Think nothing of it, my boy," said the Fox. "Seeing you happy is our only reward. Our only reward—reward—*reward!*" he kept repeating, until the wicked-looking Coachman slipped him a large sack of gold. The Fox had sold Pinocchio for gold!

Jiminy Cricket saw the Coachman crack his long blacksnake whip, and the coach start to move. The coach was drawn by eight sorrowful-looking little donkeys, who seemed to feel very badly. "Tsk! Tsk! Tsk!" they said, every time the Coachman's whip descended. But nobody could hear them because of the boys' shouting.

"Three cheers for anything," they yelled, throwing their caps into the air as the coach rolled away. "Hurray for Pleasure Island!"

Jiminy made a last desperate effort. He hopped onto the rear axle of the coach and rode along. Certain that Pinocchio was headed for disaster, the loyal little cricket went with him just the same.

The journey was an unhappy one for Jiminy. At the waterfront, the passengers boarded a ferryboat for Pleasure Island, and the little cricket suffered from seasickness during the entire voyage.

But physical discomfort was not what bothered him most. He was worried about Pinocchio, who promptly made friends with the worst boy in the crowd—a no-good named "Lampwick." Lampwick talked out of the corner of his mouth, and was very untidy. Yet Pinocchio cherished his friendship.

Jiminy tried to warn Pinocchio, but the heedless puppet refused to listen. Finally the ferry docked and the boys swarmed down the gangplank onto Pleasure Island.

Bands played loudly; wonderful circuses performed along the streets, which were paved with cookies and lined with doughnut trees. Lollipops and cupcakes grew on bushes, and fountains spouted lemonade and soda pop. The Mayor of Pleasure Island made a speech of welcome and urged the boys to enjoy themselves.

Yes, Pleasure Island seemed to be all the Fox had claimed for it, and more. Only Jiminy Cricket was skeptical. He felt that there was more to all this than appeared on the surface. But weeks went by, and seldom did Jiminy get close enough to Pinocchio to warn him. He was always in the midst of the fun, and his friend Lampwick was the ringleader of the horde of mischievous boys.

They smashed windows and burned schoolbooks; in fact they did whatever they felt like doing, no matter how destructive. They ate until they nearly burst. And always the Coachman and Mayor encouraged them to "Have a good time—while you can!"

And all the while the poor little donkeys—who performed all the hard labor on the island—looked very sad and said "Tsk! Tsk!!"

One day Pinocchio and Lampwick were lazily floating in a canoe along the Lemonade River, which flowed between the Ice Cream Mountains. Chocolate cattails grew thickly along the banks, lollipop trees drooped overhead, and the canoe was piled high with sweets.

"This is too good to be true, Lampwick," Pinocchio sighed blissfully. "I could stay here forever."

"Aw, this is kid stuff," retorted Lampwick. "Let's go where we can have some real fun!"

"Where?" asked Pinocchio curiously.

"I'll show you," said Lampwick. So they pulled the canoe up on the bank, and Lampwick then led the way to Tobacco Lane.

Here the fences were made of cigars, cigarettes and matches grew on bushes, and there were rows of cornstalks with corncob pipes on them. Lampwick lit a cigar and began smoking.

Pinocchio hesitated. Finally he picked a corncob pipe and began to puff timidly.

"Aw, you smoke like my granmudder," jeered Lampwick. "Take a big drag, Pinoke —like dis!"

Under Lampwick's instruction, Pinocchio soon found himself smoking like a chimney. Just then, along came Jiminy. How sad the little cricket felt when he saw this you will never know. While he had known for a long time that Pinocchio had fallen into evil ways, Jiminy did not realize he had sunk to such depths.

Well, he had tried everything—except force. Would that make the lad come to his senses? He decided to try. He shook his little fist angrily. "So it's come to this, has it?" he shouted. "SMOKING!"

Pinocchio gave him a careless glance. "Yeah," he answered out of the corner of his mouth, in imitation of Lampwick. "So what?"

"Just this!" Jiminy exploded. "You're making a disgusting spectacle of yourself. You're going home this minute!"

Lampwick, who had never seen Jiminy before, was curious. "Who's de insect, Pinoke?"

"Jiminy? Why, he's my conscience," explained Pinocchio.

Lampwick began to laugh. "You mean you take advice from a *beetle?*" he remarked insultingly. "Say, I can't waste time wid a sap like you. So long!" And he strolled away.

"Lampwick! Don't go!" cried Pinocchio. "Now see what you've done, Jiminy! Lampwick was my best friend!"

That was too much for the little cricket. "So *he's* your best friend," he said angrily. "Well, Pinocchio, that's the last straw. I'm through! I'm taking the next boat!"

Pinocchio hesitated but temptation was too strong. He couldn't give Lampwick up. He started off after him, full of apologies.

"Hey wait, Lampwick!" he called. "I'm coming with *you!*"

That was the end as far as Jiminy was concerned. "So he prefers to remain with that hoodlum, and allow him to insult *me*, his conscience?" he muttered. "Well, from now on he can paddle his own canoe. I'm going home!"

And he started toward the entrance gate, so upset that he did not notice how dark and forlorn Pleasure Island looked. There wasn't a boy in sight on the wide streets.

Jiminy's only thought was to get away quickly. He was just about to pound angrily on the gate when he heard voices on the other side. He tried to listen, and became conscious of a reddish glow which cast great, frightening shadows against the high stone walls. The shadows looked like prison guards, and they carried guns!

Jiminy jumped up and peered fearfully through the keyhole. In the cove, lit by flaming torches, he saw something that made his blood turn cold.

The ferryboat stood waiting, stripped of its decorations. The dock swarmed with howling, braying donkeys—fat ones and thin ones, many of whom still wore boys' hats and shoes. Huge, ape-like guards herded them into crates, assisted by the Coachman, who cracked his whip brutally over the poor donkeys' heads.

The little cricket shuddered. At last he understood the meaning of Pleasure Island. This, then, was what became of lazy, good-for-nothing boys! They made donkeys of themselves! This was Pinocchio's fate, unless—

Forgetting his anger, Jiminy leaped to the ground and started back toward Tobacco Lane. He must warn Pinocchio at once.

"Pinocchio!" he yelled. "Pinocchio!" But his cries only echoed through the empty streets.

Not far away, Pinocchio was still looking for Lampwick. He wandered unhappily past pie trees and popcorn shrubs. The island suddenly seemed strange, deserted.

Then he heard a frightened voice say, "Here I am!"

"Lampwick!" Pinocchio answered joyfully. "Where are you?"

Just then a little donkey emerged from some bushes. "Ssh!" he whispered. "Stop yelling! They'll hear us!"

Pinocchio stared. The donkey spoke in Lampwick's voice!

"This is no time for jokes," Pinocchio said crossly. "What are you doing in that donkey suit?"

"This ain't no donkey suit, Pinoke," the frightened voice replied. "*I am* a donkey!"

Pinocchio laughed. "You a donkey?" For he still thought it was a joke. "Ha ha ha! *He-Haw! He-Haw! He-Haw!*"

Pinocchio turned pale, but he couldn't stop. He was braying like a donkey!

The little donkey came closer to him. "That's the first sign of donkey fever," he whispered. "That's how I started."

"Then—then you *are* Lampwick! What happened?"

"Donkey fever," replied Lampwick, "and you've got it too!"

Pinocchio's head began to buzz like a hive of bees. He reached up and felt something horrible. Two long, hairy ears were growing out of his head!

"You've got it all right!" whispered Lampwick. "Look behind you!"

Pinocchio looked and discovered that he had a long tail. He began to tremble, and was no longer able to stand up straight. Then he found himself on all fours.

"Help! Help!" he shrieked. "Jiminy! Jiminy Cricket!"

Jiminy ran toward them, but he saw that he was too late.

"Oh! Oh! Oh me, oh my!" he groaned. "Look at you! Come on! Let's get away from here before you're a complete donkey!"

This time nobody argued with the little cricket. As he fled toward the high stone wall, Pinocchio and the donkey that had once been Lampwick followed as fast as their legs would carry them. But as they rounded a corner, they came face to face with the Coachman and his armed guards. They turned and dashed toward the opposite wall.

"There they go! That's the two that's missing!" yelled the Coachman. "After them! Sound the alarm!"

Instantly the air was filled with the sound of sirens and the baying of bloodhounds. Searchlights began to play over the island, and bullets whizzed past the ears of the escaping prisoners. They expected any minute to be shot.

Pinocchio and Jiminy reached the wall and managed to climb to the top before the ape-like guards got within shooting distance. But Lampwick, with his donkey hoofs, could not climb.

"Go on, Pinoke!" he cried. "It's all over with me!"

A lump came in Pinocchio's throat. After all, Lampwick was his friend. But there was nothing he could do. He turned his back and said a silent prayer. Then he and Jiminy dove into the sea.

Bullets splashed all around them in the

water, but by some miracle neither of them was hit. Finally a thick fog hid them from the glaring searchlights, and the sound of the guns died away. They had escaped!

It was a long, hard swim back to the mainland. When they reached shore,

Pinocchio longed to see once more the cozy little cottage and his dear, kind father. Pleasure Island, and all it stood for, now seemed like a bad dream. But they were by no means at the end of their journey, for home was still many weary miles away.

It was winter when at last one evening they limped into the village. They hurried through the drifting snow to Geppetto's shop. Eagerly, Pinocchio pounded on the door.

"Father! Father!" he cried. "It's me! It's Pinocchio!"

But the only reply was the howling of the wintry wind.

"He must be asleep," said Pinocchio, and he knocked again. But again there was no answer.

Worried, Pinocchio hastened to the window and peered in. The house was empty! Everything was shrouded and dusty.

"He's gone, Jiminy," said Pinocchio sorrowfully. "My father's gone away!"

"Looks like he's gone for good, too," said Jiminy. "What'll we do?"

"I don't know." Pinocchio sat down on the doorstep shivering. A tear came from his eye, ran down his long nose and froze into a tiny, sparkling icicle. But Pinocchio didn't even bother to wipe it off. He felt terrible.

Just then a gust of wind blew around the corner, carrying a piece of paper. Jiminy hopped over to see what it was.

"Hey, Pinoke, it's a letter!" he exclaimed.

"Oh! Maybe it's from my father!" cried Pinocchio, and he quickly took the note from Jiminy and tried to read it. But alas, the marks on the paper meant nothing.

"You see, if you had gone to school you could read your father's letter," Jiminy reminded him. "Here—give it to me!"

The little cricket began to read the note aloud, and this is what it said:

"Dear Pinocchio:

"I heard you had gone to Pleasure Island, so I got a small boat and started off to search for you. Everyone said it was a dangerous voyage, but Figaro, Cleo, and I thought we could reach you and save you from a terrible fate.

"We weathered the storms, and finally reached the Terrible Straits. But just as we came in sight of our goal, out of the sea rose Monstro, the Terror of the Deep—the giant whale who swallows ships whole. He opened his jaws. In we went—boat and all . . .''

Here Pinocchio's sobs interrupted Jiminy's reading of the letter as he realized Geppetto's plight.

"Oh, my poor, poor father!" the puppet moaned. "He's dead! And it's all my fault!" He began to weep bitterly.

"But he isn't dead!" said Jiminy, and read on.

"So now, dear son, we are living at the bottom of the ocean in the belly of the whale. But there is very little to eat here, and we cannot exist much longer. So I fear you will never again see

Your loving father, GEPPETTO."

"Hurrah! Hurrah!" shouted Pinocchio.

"Hurrah for what?" asked Jiminy somewhat crossly. It did not seem to him to be quite the time for cheers.

"Don't you see, Jiminy?" cried Pinocchio. "My father is still alive! There may be time to save him!"

"Save him?" said Jiminy stupidly. Then suddenly a light dawned. "You don't mean *you*—"

"Yes!" announced Pinocchio. "I'm going after him. It's my fault he's down there in the whale; I'm going to the bottom of the ocean to rescue him!"

"But Pinocchio, you might be killed!" warned the cricket.

"I don't mind," declared Pinocchio. "What does life mean to me without my father? I've got to save him!"

Jiminy stared with open mouth. He hardly recognized this new Pinocchio—a brave, unselfish Pinocchio who stood there in place of the weak, foolish puppet he had always known.

"But think how far it is to the seashore—" he began.

Pinocchio looked thoughtful, but not for long. "I don't care. No place is too far for me to go after my father."

Just then, with a flutter of wings, a beautiful white dove settled gracefully down in the snow beside them.

"I will take you to the seashore," she said.

"You?" Pinocchio stared. But he did not see the tiny gold crown on the dove's head. It was she who had dropped the letter from the sky. She was his own dear Blue Fairy, disguised as a dove.

"Yes, I will help you," she assured him.

"How could a little dove carry me to the seashore?"

"Like this!"

And the dove began to grow and grow, until she was larger than an eagle. "Jump on my back," she commanded. Pinocchio obeyed.

"Good-bye, Jiminy Cricket," he said. "I may never see you again." He waved his hand to his little friend. "Thank you for all you've done!"

"Good-bye, nothing!" retorted Jiminy, and he too jumped on the back of the great white dove. "You're not leaving me! We'll see this through together!"

The dove raised her wide wings and rose from the ground. Higher and higher they flew, till the village disappeared and all they could see beneath them was whirling snow.

All night they flew through the storm. When morning came, the sun shone brightly. The dove's wings slowed down and she glided to earth at the edge of a cliff. Far below, the sea lay churning and lashing like a restless giant.

"I can take you no farther," said the dove. "Are you quite sure you want to go on this dangerous mission?"

"Yes," said Pinocchio. "Thank you for the ride. Good-bye!"

"Good-bye, Pinocchio," the dove replied. "Good luck!"

And she grew small again and flew away. Neither Pinocchio nor Jiminy realized that she was the Blue Fairy, but they were very grateful.

As soon as the dove was out of sight, Pinocchio tied a big stone to his donkey tail, to anchor him to the floor of the ocean. Then he smiled bravely at Jiminy and together they leaped off the cliff.

The weight of the stone caused Pinocchio to sink at once. By clinging desperately, little Jiminy managed to stay close by. They landed, picked themselves up and peered about. They were at the very bottom of the sea.

At first it seemed dark; they were many fathoms deep. Gradually Pinocchio's eyes became accustomed to the greenish light which filtered down into the submarine forest.

Giant clumps of seaweed waved overhead, like the branches of trees. Among them darted lovely bright objects, like birds or living flowers. They soon saw that these brilliant creatures were fish of all descriptions.

However, Pinocchio was in no frame of mind to make a study of the citizens of the sea. He walked along, peering into every cave and grotto in search of the great whale.

But the stone attached to his tail made him move slowly, and he grew impatient.

"I wish we knew just where to look," he thought. "Jiminy, where do you suppose Monstro might be?"

"Don't know, I'm sure," replied Jiminy. "I'll inquire here."

He knocked politely on an oyster. Its shell opened.

"Pardon me, Pearl," Jiminy began, "but could you tell me where we might find Monstro the Whale?"

To his surprise, the shell closed with a sharp click and the oyster scuttled off into a kelp bush as though frightened.

"Hm! That's funny!" remarked Jiminy.

Just then a school of tropical fish approached, brightly beautiful and extremely curious.

"I wonder," Pinocchio began, "if you could tell me where to find Monstro—"

But the lovely little creatures darted away before he had finished speaking. It was as though Pinocchio had threatened to harm them in some way.

A bit farther along, they encountered a herd of tiny sea horses, grazing on the sandy bottom. Pinocchio tried once more.

"Could you tell me," he asked, "where I might find Monstro the Whale?"

But the sea horses fled, their little ears raised in alarm.

"You know what I think?" exclaimed Jiminy. "I think everybody down here is afraid of Monstro! Why, they run away at the very mention of his name! He must be awful. Do you think we should go on?"

"Certainly!" declared Pinocchio. "I'm not afraid!"

So they went on. It was a strange journey. Sometimes the water grew very dark, and tiny phosphorescent fish glowed like fireflies in the depths. They learned to be careful not to step on the huge flowers which lay on the ocean's floor. For they were not flowers but sea anemones, which could reach up and capture whatever came within their grasp.

Striped fish glared at them from seaweed thickets like tigers in a jungle, and fish with horns and quills glowered at them. They saw wonders of the deep which no human eye has ever beheld—but nowhere could they find so much as one clue to the whereabouts of Monstro, the Terror of the Deep.

"The time is getting short!" said Pinocchio at last. "We must find him! My father will starve to death!"

"Father," he cried desperately. But there was no sound except the constant shifting and sighing of the watery depths.

"Let's go home, Pinocchio," Jiminy pleaded. "We'll never find Monstro in this big place. For all we know, we may be looking in the wrong ocean."

"No, Jiminy," said Pinocchio, "I'll never give up! Never!"

Not far away lay the Terror of the Deep, floating close to the surface, fast asleep. At times his broad back rose out of the water, to be mistaken for a desert island.

It was lucky for any ship close by that Monstro slept, for with but one flip of his tail he had been known to crush the sturdiest craft. As he snored the roars sounded like a tempest. It seemed impossible that anything could live within those crushing jaws.

Yet at the far end of the long, dark cavern formed by the whale's mouth lived a strange household: a kindly old man, whose skin was as pale as white paper, a small black kitten, whose ribs nearly pierced his fur, and a tiny, frightened goldfish, who swam weakly around in her bowl.

The old woodcarver had made his home on a shipwreck and furnished it with broken packing-cases from ships the whale had swallowed. He had salvaged a lantern, pots and pans and a few other necessities of life. But his stock of food was now very low; the lantern sputtering above his table was almost out of oil. The end was near.

Every day he fished in the mouth of the whale; but when Monstro slept, nothing entered that dark cavern. Now there was only a shallow pool of water, and it was useless to fish.

"Not a bite for days, Figaro," Geppetto said. "If Monstro doesn't wake up soon, it will be too bad for us. I never thought it would end like this!" He sighed mournfully. "Here we are, starving in the belly of a whale. And Pinocchio—poor, dear, little Pinocchio!" Geppetto was obliged to raise his thin voice to a shout, to be heard above the whale's snoring.

The old woodcarver looked tired and worn. He had never been so hungry in his whole life. Figaro was hungry too. He stared greedily at little Cleo, swimming slowly about her bowl.

As Geppetto went wearily back to his fishing, the kitten began to sneak toward Cleo's bowl. But the old man saw him.

"Scat!" shouted Geppetto. "You beast! You dog! Shame on you, Figaro, chasing Cleo, after the way I've brought you up!"

The hungry kitten scuttled away to a corner to try to forget the pangs whch gnawed him. Just then Geppetto felt a nibble at his line. He pulled it up in great excitement.

"It's a package, Figaro!" he cried. "Maybe it's food. Sausage, or cheese—"

But when the water-soaked package was unwrapped, it contained only a cook book! What a grim trick Fate had played!

"Oh, oh," groaned Geppetto. "I am so hungry! If we only had something to cook! Anything—"

He turned the pages, his mouth watering at the pictured recipes. "101 Ways to Cook

Fish," he read. Suddenly his eyes were drawn, as if by a magnet, to Cleo. He could almost see the melted butter sizzling! As in a nightmare, he walked toward the goldfish.

But as he started to scoop his little pet out and put her in the frying pan, the old man realized he could never do this thing.

"Dear Cleo," he begged, "forgive me! If we must die, let us die as we have lived—friends through thick and thin!"

It was a solemn moment. All felt that the end was near.

Then the whale moved!

"He's waking up!" cried Geppetto. "He's opening his mouth!"

Monstro gave an upward lunge, and through his jaws rushed a wall of black water. With it came fish—a whole school of fish! Hundreds of them.

"Food!" yelled Geppetto, seizing his pole. "Tuna fish! Oh, Figaro, Cleo—we are saved!"

And he began to pull fish after fish out of the water.

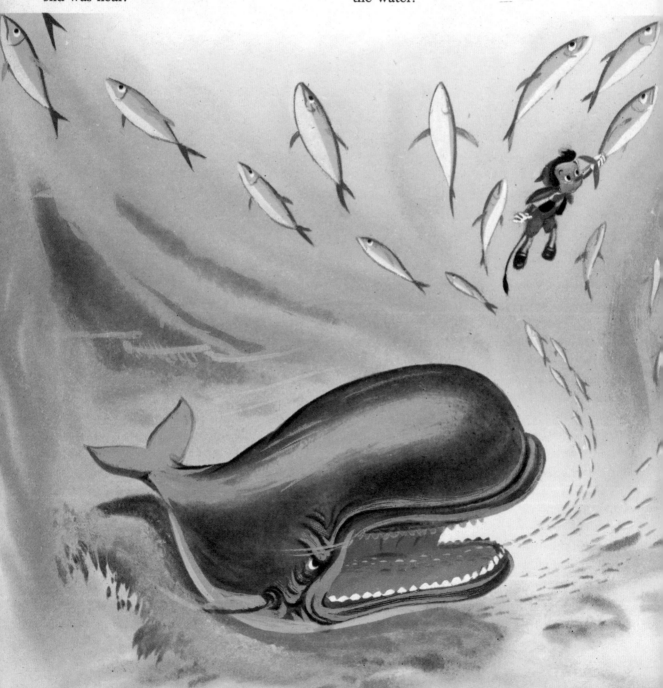

When Monstro woke, opened his eyes and saw the school of tuna approaching, he threshed the ocean into turmoil for miles around.

Pinocchio noticed every creature in the sea taking flight, but he did not understand the reason until he saw the whale coming toward him. Then he *knew*.

"Monstro!" he shrieked. "Jiminy, swim for your life!" For although he had long been in search of the Terror of the Deep, a mere look at those crushing jaws was enough to make him flee in terror.

But nothing in Monstro's path could escape. He swallowed hundreds of tuna at one gulp. Into that huge maw finally went Pinocchio!

At last, completely satisfied, the whale grunted and settled down for another nap.

"Blubber-mouth!" cried a shrill, small voice. "Let me in!"

It was Jiminy, clinging to an empty bottle, bobbing up and down outside Monstro's jaws, begging to be swallowed too.

But the whale paid no attention, except to settle farther into the water. The little cricket was left alone, except for a flock of seagulls who began to swoop down and peck at him. He raised his umbrella and drove them away, got inside the bottle and prepared to wait for Pinocchio.

Inside the whale, although Geppetto's bin was already heaped, he was still at work pulling in tuna.

"There's enough food to last us for months," he told Figaro joyfully. "Wait, there's another big one!" He scarcely noticed a shrill little cry of "Father!"

"Pinocchio?" the old man asked himself in wonderment, and rubbed his eyes. There, standing before him, was his boy! "Pinocchio!" he exclaimed joyfully. "Are my eyes telling me the truth? Are you really my own dear Pinocchio?"

Geppetto was not the only one who was glad. Figaro licked Pinocchio's face, and little Cleo turned somersaults.

"You see, we have all missed you," said Geppetto fondly. "But you're sneezing! You've caught cold, son! You should not have come down here! Sit down and rest! Give me your hat!"

But when Pinocchio's hat was removed, those hated donkey ears popped out into plain sight. .

"Pinocchio!" cried Geppetto, shocked. *"Those ears!"*

Pinocchio hung his head in shame. "I've got a tail, too," he admitted sadly. *"Oh, Father!"* And he turned his head away to hide his tears.

"Never mind, son," Geppetto comforted

him. "The main thing is that we are all to-gether again."

Pinocchio brightened up. "The *main* thing is to figure out a way to get out!"

"I've tried everything," said Geppetto hopelessly. "I even built a raft—"

"That's it!" cried Pinocchio. "When he opens his mouth, we'll float out on the raft!"

"Oh, no," argued Geppetto. "When he opens his mouth everything comes in—nothing goes out. Come, we are all hungry—I will cook a fish dinner! Help me build a fire—"

"That's it, Father!" interrupted Pinocchio. "We'll build a great big fire!" And he began to throw into the fire everything he could get his hands on.

"Not the chairs!" warned Geppetto. "What will we sit on?"

"We won't need chairs," shouted Pinocchio. "We'll build a big fire and make Monstro sneeze! When he sneezes, out we go! Hurry—more wood!"

As the fire began to smoke they got the raft ready.

"It won't work, son," Geppetto insisted mournfully.

But before long the whale began to grunt and cough. Suddenly he drew in his breath and gave a monstrous SNEEZE! Out went the raft, past those crushing jaws, into the sea.

"We made it!" shouted Pinocchio. "Father, we're free!"

But they were not yet free. The angry whale saw them and plunged ferociously after their frail raft. He hit it squarely, splintering it into thousands of pieces. Pinocchio and Geppetto swam for their lives, with Monstro, the Terror of the Deep, in full pursuit.

The old man clung weakly to a board. He knew he could never reach land, but there was still hope for Pinocchio.

"Save yourself, my boy!" cried Geppetto. "Swim for shore, and don't worry about me!"

But the brave puppet swam to his father and managed to keep him afloat. Giant waves swept them toward the dark, forbidding rocks which lined the shore. Even if they escaped Monstro, they would surely be crushed to death.

But between two of the rocks there was a small, hidden crevice. By some miracle, Pinocchio and Geppetto were washed through this crevice into a small, sheltered lagoon. Again and again the furious whale threw his bulk against the rocks on the other side. His quarry had escaped!

But alas, when Geppetto sat up dizzily he saw poor Pinocchio lying motionless beside him, still and pale. The heartbroken old man knelt and wept bitterly, certain his wooden boy was dead.

The gentle waves carried a fishbowl up onto the beach. It was Cleo—and to the edge of the bowl clung a bedraggled kitten, Figaro. But even they were no comfort to Geppetto now.

A bottle bobbed up out of the water. Inside it rode Jiminy Cricket. He saw what had happened and longed to comfort Geppetto, but his own heart was broken.

The sorrowful old man finally gathered poor Pinocchio in his arms, picked up his pets and started home. They too felt sad, for they knew Geppetto was lonelier than he had ever been before.

When they reached home, it no longer seemed a home; it was dark and cheerless. Geppetto put Pinocchio on the workbench, buried his face in his hands and prayed.

Suddenly a ray of starlight pierced the gloom. It sought out the lifeless figure of the puppet. A voice which seemed to come from the sky said, as it had said once before:

"—and some day, when you have proven yourself brave, truthful and unselfish, you will be a real boy—"

The old man saw and heard nothing. But Pinocchio stirred, sat up and looked around. He saw the others grieving, and wondered why. Then he looked down at himself, felt of his arms and legs, and suddenly he realized what had happened.

"Father!" he cried. "Father, look at me!"

Pinocchio was alive—really alive. No longer a wooden puppet, but a real flesh-and-blood boy!

Geppetto stared unbelievingly. Once more he picked Pinocchio up in his arms and hugged him, and cried—this time for joy. Again a miracle had been performed; this was truly the answer to his wish—the son he had always wanted!

What did they do to celebrate? Geppetto made a fire and soon the house was as warm and cozy as ever. He started all the clocks and played the music box. Figaro turned somersaults, and Cleo raced madly about her bowl. Pinocchio flew to get his precious toys; even they seemed gayer than ever.

As for Jiminy Cricket, he was the happiest and proudest of all. For on his lapel he now wore a beautiful badge of shining gold!

MOTHER GOOSE

JACK AND JILL

Jack and Jill went up the hill
   To fetch a pail of water.
Jack fell down and broke his crown
   And Jill came tumbling after.

Up Jack got, and home did trot
   As fast as he could caper,
Went to bed and plastered his head
   With vinegar and brown paper.

HICKETY, PICKETY

Hickety, pickety, my black hen,
She lays eggs for gentlemen;
Gentlemen come every day
To see what my black hen doth lay.

DING, DONG, BELL

Ding, dong, bell,
Pussy's in the well!
Who put her in?—
Little Johnny Green.
Who pulled her out?—
Big Johnny Stout.
What a naughty boy was that
To try to drown poor pussy cat,
Who never did him any harm,
But killed the mice in his father's barn.

A DILLAR, A DOLLAR

A dillar, a dollar,
A ten o'clock scholar,
What makes you come so soon?
You used to come at ten o'clock,
And now you come at noon.

OLD KING COLE

Old King Cole was a merry old soul,
　　And a merry old soul was he;
He called for his pipes and he called for his bowl,
　　And he called for his fiddlers three!

Every fiddler he had a fine fiddle,
　　And a very fine fiddle had he;
Twee-tweedle-dee, tweedle-dee, went the fiddlers.
Oh, there's none so rare as can compare
　　With King Cole and his fiddlers three!

CROSS PATCH

Cross patch,
Draw the latch,
Sit by the fire and spin;
Take a cup
And drink it up,
And call your neighbors in.

LITTLE BOY BLUE

Little Boy Blue, come blow your horn;
The sheep's in the meadow, the cow's in the corn.
Where's the boy that looks after the sheep?
He's under the haystack, fast asleep.

THE JOLLY MILLER

There was a jolly miller
  Lived on the river Dee;
He worked and sang from morn till night
  No lark so blithe as he.
And this the burden of his song
  Forever used to be—
"I care for nobody—no, not I,
  Since nobody cares for me."

DOCTOR FOSTER

Doctor Foster went to Gloucester,
  In a shower of rain;
He stepped in a puddle up to his middle,
  And never went there again.

LITTLE JACK HORNER

Little Jack Horner sat in a corner,
Eating a Christmas pie;
He put in his thumb, and took out a plum,
And said, "What a good boy am I!"

GEORGIE PORGIE

Georgie Porgie, pudding and pie,
Kissed the girls and made them cry.
When the boys came out to play
Georgie Porgie ran away.

THREE WISE MEN
OF GOTHAM

Three wise men of Gotham
Went to sea in a bowl;
If the bowl had been stronger,
My song had been longer.

THE OLD WOMAN
WHO LIVED IN A SHOE

There was an old woman who lived in a shoe;
She had so many children she didn't know what to do.
She gave them some broth, without any bread;
She whipped them all soundly and sent them to bed.

SIMPLE SIMON

Simple Simon met a pieman,
Going to the fair;
Says Simple Simon to the pieman,
"Let me taste your ware."

Says the pieman to Simple Simon,
"Show me first your penny."
Says Simple Simon to the pieman,
"Indeed I have not any."

He went to catch a dickey-bird,
  And thought he could not fail,
Because he'd got a little salt
  To put upon his tail.

Simple Simon went a-fishing,
  For to catch a whale;
All the water he had got
  Was in his mother's pail.

He went for water in a sieve,
  But soon it all ran through;
And now poor Simple Simon
  Bids you all adieu.

LITTLE MISS MUFFET

Little Miss Muffet
Sat on a tuffet,
Eating her curds and whey.
There came a great spider,
And sat down beside her,
And frightened Miss Muffet away!

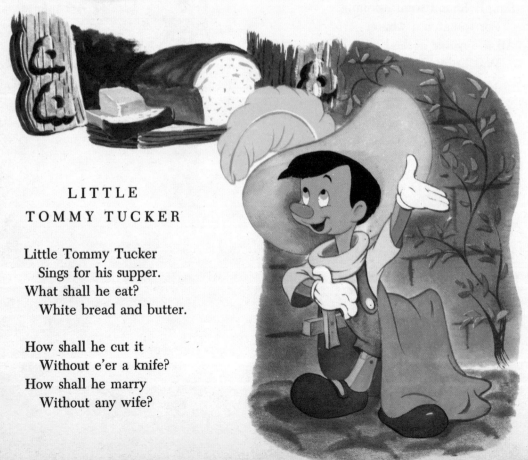

LITTLE
TOMMY TUCKER

Little Tommy Tucker
  Sings for his supper.
What shall he eat?
  White bread and butter.

How shall he cut it
  Without e'er a knife?
How shall he marry
  Without any wife?

RUB A DUB DUB

Rub a dub dub,
Three men in a tub,
And who do you think they be?
The butcher, the baker,
The candlestick maker.
Turn 'em out, knaves all three.

ROCK-A-BYE, BABY

Rock-a-bye, baby,
On the tree top!
When the wind blows,
The cradle will rock;
When the bough breaks,
The cradle will fall;
Down will come baby,
Cradle and all.

ONE TO TEN

1, 2, 3, 4, 5,
I caught a hare alive;
6, 7, 8, 9, 10,
I let him go again.

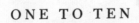

MISTRESS MARY

Mistress Mary, quite contrary,
How does your garden grow?
With silver bells and cockle shells
And pretty maids all in a row.

BAA, BAA, BLACK SHEEP

Baa, baa, black sheep, have you any wool?
Yes, sir, yes, sir, three bags full;
One for my master, one for my dame,
And one for the little boy who cries in the lane.

JACK BE NIMBLE

Jack be nimble,
Jack be quick,
Jack jump over
The candlestick.

WEE WILLIE WINKIE

Wee Willie Winkie runs through the town,
Upstairs and downstairs, in his night-gown;
Rapping at the window, crying at the lock,
"Are the babies in their beds, for now it's eight o'clock!"

BYE, BABY BUNTING

Bye, baby bunting,
Daddy's gone a-hunting,
To get a little rabbit's skin
To wrap the baby bunting in.

255

LITTLE BETTY BLUE

Little Betty Blue
　　Lost her holiday shoe.
What shall little Betty do?
　　Buy her another
To match the other,
　　And then she'll walk in two.

JUMPING JOAN

Here am I, little Jumping Joan.
When nobody's with me,
I'm always alone.

DEEDLE, DEEDLE DUMPLING

Deedle, deedle dumpling, my son John,
Went to bed with his stockings on;
One shoe off and one shoe on,
Deedle, deedle dumpling, my son John.

PUSSY CAT, WHERE HAVE
YOU BEEN?

"Pussy cat, pussy cat, where have you been?"
"I've been to London to look at the Queen."
"Pussy cat, pussy cat, what did you there?"
"I frightened a little mouse under her chair."

256

THIS LITTLE PIG

This little pig went to market,
This little pig stayed at home,
This little pig had roast beef,
This little pig had none,
This little pig cried, "Wee-wee-wee!"
All the way home.

257

RIDE A COCK HORSE

Ride a cock horse to Banbury Cross
To see a fine lady upon a white horse.
Rings on her fingers, and bells on her toes,
She shall have music wherever she goes.

PETER, PETER, PUMPKIN EATER

Peter, Peter, pumpkin-eater,
Had a wife and couldn't keep her;
He put her in a pumpkin shell,
And there he kept her very well.

MARY'S LAMB

Mary had a little lamb,
  Its fleece was white as snow;
And everywhere that Mary went,
  The lamb was sure to go.

It followed her to school one day;
  Which was against the rule;
It made the children laugh and play
  To see a lamb at school.

JACK SPRAT

Jack Sprat could eat no fat,
  His wife could eat no lean;
And so betwixt them both, you see,
  They licked the platter clean.

259

HARK, HARK

Hark, hark,
The dogs do bark,
The beggars are coming to town;
  Some in rags,
  Some in bags,
And some in velvet gowns.

HOT CROSS BUNS

Hot cross buns!
Hot cross buns!
One a penny, two a penny,
Hot cross buns!

If you have no daughters,
Give them to your sons.
One a penny, two a penny,
Hot cross buns!

IF I'D AS MUCH MONEY

If I'd as much money as I could spend,
I never would cry old chairs to mend,
Old chairs to mend, old chairs to mend—
I never would cry old chairs to mend.

If I'd as much money as I could tell,
I never would cry old clothes to sell,
Old clothes to sell, old clothes to sell—
I never would cry old clothes to sell.

HEY, DIDDLE, DIDDLE

Hey, diddle, diddle, the cat and the fiddle,
The cow jumped over the moon;
The little dog laughed to see such sport,
And the dish ran away with the spoon.

CURLY LOCKS

Curly Locks! Curly Locks! Wilt thou be mine?
Thou shalt not wash dishes, nor yet feed the swine,
But sit on a cushion and sew a fine seam,
And feed upon strawberries, sugar, and cream!

LITTLE TOMMY TITTLEMOUSE

Little Tommy Tittlemouse
Lived in a little house;
He caught fishes
In other men's ditches.

BOBBY SHAFTOE

Bobby Shaftoe's gone to sea,
Silver buckles at his knee;
He'll come back and marry me,—
Pretty Bobby Shaftoe!

THERE WERE TWO BLACKBIRDS

There were two blackbirds,
    Sitting on a hill,
The one named Jack,
    The other named Jill.

Fly away, Jack!
    Fly away, Jill!
Come again, Jack!
    Come again, Jill!

SING A SONG OF SIXPENCE

Sing a song of sixpence, a pocket full of rye,
Four and twenty blackbirds, baked in a pie;
When the pie was opened, the birds began to sing;
Wasn't that a dainty dish to set before the king?

The king was in the parlor, counting out his money,
The queen was in the kitchen, eating bread and honey;
The maid was in the garden, hanging out the clothes,
When along came a blackbird, and nipped off her nose.

PAT-A-CAKE

Pat-a-cake, pat-a-cake,
  Baker's man.
Bake me a cake,
  As fast as you can.
Pat it and prick it
  And mark it with B.
Put it in the oven
  For Baby and me.

THERE WAS AN OLD WOMAN

There was an old woman tossed up in a basket,
  Seventeen times as high as the moon;
And where she was going, I couldn't but ask it,
  For in her hand she carried a broom.

"Old woman, old woman, old woman," said I,
  "O whither, O whither, O whither so high?"
"To sweep the cobwebs off the sky!"
  "Shall I go with you?" "Yes, by and by."

GRANDPA BUNNY

Deep in the woods where the brier bushes grow, lies Bunnyville, a busy little bunny rabbit town.

And in the very center of that busy little town stands a cottage, a neat twig cottage, with a neat brown roof, which is known to all as the very own home of Great Grandpa Bunny Bunny.

Great Grandpa Bunny Bunny, as every bunny knows, was the ancestral founder of the town, which is a very fine thing to be.

He liked to tell the young bunnies who always gathered around how he and Mrs. Bunny Bunny, when they were very young, had found that very brier patch and built themselves that very same little twig house.

It was a happy life they lived there, deep in the woods, bringing up their bunny family in that little house of twigs.

And of course Daddy Bunny Bunny, as he was called then, was busy at his job, decorating Easter eggs.

As the children grew up, they helped paint Easter eggs. And soon the children were all grown up, with families of their own. And they built a ring of houses all around their parents' home.

By and by they had a town there, and they called it Bunnyville.

Now Grandpa Bunny Bunny had lots of help painting Easter eggs—so much that he began to look for other jobs to do.

He taught some of the young folks to paint flowers in the woods.

They tried out some new shades of green on mosses and on ferns.

They made those woods so beautiful that people who went walking there marveled at the wonderful colors.

"The soil must be especially rich," they said, "or the rainfall especially wet."

And the bunnies would hear them and silently laugh. For they knew it was all their Grandpa Bunny Bunny's doing.

Years went by. Now there were still more families in Bunnyville. And Grandpa Bunny Bunny had grown to be Great Grandpa Bunny Bunny. For that is how things go. He still supervised all the Easter egg painting, and the work on the flowers every spring.

But he had *so* much help that between times he looked around for other jobs to do.

He taught some of the bunnies to paint the autumn leaves—purple for the gum trees, yellow for the elms, patterns in scarlet for the sugar maple trees. Through the woods they went with their brushes and their pails.

And the people who went walking there would say among themselves, "Never has there been such color in these woods. The nights, in these woods, must have been especially frosty."

And the bunnies would hear them and silently laugh. For they knew that it was all their Great Grandpa's plan.

And so it went, as the seasons rolled around. There were constantly more bunnies in that busy Bunnyville.

And Great Grandpa was busy finding jobs for them to do.

He taught them in winter to paint shadows on the snow and pictures in frost on wintry window panes and to polish up the diamond lights on glittering icicles.

And between times he told stories to each crop of bunny young, around the cozy fire in his neat little twig home. The bunny children loved him and his funny bunny tales. And they loved the new and different things he found for them to do.

But at last it did seem as if he'd thought of everything! He had crews of bunnies trained to paint the first tiny buds of spring.

He had teams who waited beside cocoons to touch up the wings of new butterflies.

Some specialized in beetles, some in creeping, crawling things.

They had painted up that whole wild wood till it sparkled and it gleamed.

And now, the bunnies wondered, what would he think of next? Well, Great Grandpa stayed at home a lot those days, and thought and thought. At last he told a secret to that season's bunny boys and girls.

"Children," Great Grandpa Bunny Bunny said, "I am going to go away. And I'll tell you what my next job will be, if you'll promise not to say."

So the bunny children promised. And Great Grandpa went away. The older bunnies missed him, and often they looked sad. But the bunny children only smiled and looked extremely wise. For they knew a secret they had promised not to tell.

Then one day a windy rainstorm pelted down on Bunnyville. Everyone scampered speedily home and stayed cozy and dry in the cottages.

After a while the rain slowed down to single dripping drops.

Then every front door opened, and out the bunny children ran.

"Oh, it's true!" those bunnies shouted. And they did a bunny dance. "Great Grandpa Bunny Bunny has been at work again. Come see what he has done!"

And the people walking out that day looked up in pleased surprise.

"Have you ever," they cried, "simply *ever* seen a sunset so gorgeously bright?"

The little bunnies heard them and they chuckled silently. For they knew that it was the secret. It was all Great Grandpa Bunny Bunny's plan.

THE THREE
LITTLE PIGS

ONCE UPON A TIME there were three little pigs who went out into the big world to build their homes and seek their fortunes.

The first little pig did not like to work at all. He quickly built himself a house of straw. Then he danced down the road, to see how his brothers were getting along.

The second little pig was building himself a house, too. He did not like to work any better than his brother. So the second little pig decided to build a quick and easy house of sticks.

Soon it was finished, too. It was not a very strong little house, but at least the work was done. Now the second little pig was free to do what he liked.

What he liked to do was to play his fiddle and dance. So while the first little pig tooted his flute, the second little pig sawed away on his fiddle, dancing as he played.

And as he danced he sang:

> *"I built my house of sticks,*
> *I built my house of twigs.*
> *With a hey diddle-diddle*
> *I play on my fiddle,*
> *And dance all kinds of jigs."*

Then off danced the two little pigs down the road together to see how their brother was getting along.

The third little pig was a sober little pig. He was building his house of bricks. He did not mind hard work, and he wanted a stout little, strong little house, for he knew that in the woods nearby there lived a big bad wolf who loved to eat up little pigs.

So slap, slosh, slap! Away he worked, laying bricks and smoothing mortar.

"Ha ha ha!" laughed the first little pig, when he saw his brother hard at work.

"Ho ho ho!" laughed the second little pig. "Come down and play with us!" he called to the third little pig.

But the busy little pig did not pause. Slap, slosh, slap! Away he worked, laying bricks as he called down to his brothers:

> *I build my house of stones.*
> *I build my house of bricks.*
> *I have no chance*
> *To sing and dance,*
> *For work and play don't mix.*"

"Ho ho ho! Ha ha ha!" laughed the two lazy little pigs, dancing along to the tune of the fiddle and the flute.

"You can laugh and dance and sing," their busy brother called after them, "but I'll be safe and you'll be sorry when the wolf comes."

"Ha ha ha! Ho ho ho!" laughed the two little pigs again, and they disappeared into the woods singing a merry tune:

"Who's afraid of the big bad wolf,
The big bad wolf, the big bad wolf?
Who's afraid of the big bad wolf?
Tra la la la la-a-a-a!"

Just as the first pig reached his door, out of the woods popped the big bad wolf! The little pig squealed with fright.

"Little pig, little pig, let me come in!" cried the big bad wolf.

"Not by the hair on my chinny-chin-chin!" said the little pig.

"Then I'll huff and I'll puff and I'll blow your house in!" roared the wolf.

And he did. He blew the little straw house all to pieces!

Away raced the little pig to his brother's house of sticks. No sooner was he in the door, when knock, knock, knock! There was the big bad wolf! But of course, the little pigs would not let him come in.

"I'll fool them," said the wolf. He left the little pig's house, and he hid behind a tree.

Soon the door opened and the two little pigs peeked out. There was no wolf in sight.

"Ha ha ha! Ho ho ho!" laughed the two little pigs. "We fooled him."

Then they danced around the room, singing gaily:

*"Who's afraid of the big bad wolf,
    The big bad wolf, the big bad wolf?
Who's afraid of the big bad wolf?
    Tra la la la la-a-a-a!"*

Soon there came another knock at the door. It was the big bad wolf again, but he had covered himself with a sheepskin, and was curled up in a big basket, looking like a little lamb.

"Who's there?" called the second little pig.

"I'm a poor little sheep, with no place to sleep. Please open the door and let me in," said the big bad wolf in a sweet little voice.

The little pig peeked through a crack of the door, and he could see the wolf's big black paws and sharp fangs.

"Not by the hair of my chinny-chin-chin!"

"You can't fool us with that sheepskin!" said the second little pig.

"Then I'll huff, and I'll puff, and I'll blow your house in!" cried the angry old wolf.

So he huffed
  and he PUFFED
    and he puffed
      and he HUFFED,
and he blew the little twig house all to pieces!

Away raced the two little pigs, straight to the third little pig s house of bricks.

"Don't worry," said the third little pig to his two frightened little brothers. "You are safe here." Soon they were all singing gaily.

This made the wolf perfectly furious!

"Now by the hair of my chinny-chin-chin!" he roared. "I'll huff, and I'll puff, and I'll blow your house in!"

So the big bad wolf huffed and he PUFFED, and he puffed and he HUFFED, but he could not blow down that little house of bricks! How could he get in? At last he thought of the chimney!

So up he climbed, quietly. Then with a snarl, down he jumped—right into a kettle of boiling water!

With a yelp of pain he sprang straight up the chimney again, and raced away into the woods. The three little pigs never saw him again, and spent their time in the strong little brick house singing and dancing merrily.

BONGO

BONGO was a circus bear, a smart and lively circus bear. He was the smartest little bear any circus ever had. Yes, Bongo was the star of the show!

When the drums went tr-r-rum, and the bugles shouted, that was the signal for Bongo's act. Then the spotlights all pointed their long fingers of light down at an opening in the tent, and in rode Bongo!

In rode Bongo on his shiny unicycle, all aglitter under the glare of the lights. And his act began.

He juggled and danced on the highest trapeze. He walked a tightrope with the greatest of ease. Then up, up, up to the top of the tent went Bongo. And when he'd gone so high that he couldn't go higher, he rode his unicycle daringly on the high tight wire!

"Hurray for Bongo!" he heard voices call below.

"You know, he's the star who makes the show!"

Bongo was king of the circus while his act was on!

But when it was over, and Bongo the star rode out of the ring to the roar of applause, then clang went an iron collar around his neck. Rattle went a long chain as Bongo was led away to his boxcar. Slam went the barred door as it locked behind him. There sat Bongo, the star of the circus, just a bear in a gilded cage.

Poor Bongo! Oh, he was well enough treated. He was fed only the finest selected bear food, from his own tin dishes. He always had fresh water to drink. He was washed and combed and curried and clipped, and kept in the very finest condition.

But after all was said and done, he was still just a slave. He was lonely, too. And from somewhere deep in his past, the voice of the wild called to him.

"Bongo, Bongo, yoo-hoo, Bongo!" it sang.

He heard it in the scream of the train whistle, as the circus moved from town to town. He heard it in the clatter of the speeding wheels.

Each time the circus stopped in a new town Bongo went through his act as though he were in a dream. And when he was put back into his cage he lived in that dream—a dream of the wide-open spaces.

The voice of the wild kept calling, "Bongo!"

One day that call got into his blood so that he could not sit still. He paced around his cage as it jolted with the motion of the train. He shook the bars. He hammered at the door. And the boxcar door swung open!

Bongo was face to face with the great out-of-doors.

The train was moving slowly around a curve. Quickly Bongo swung out on his little cycle, dropped to the roadbed, and zipped away down a long hillside.

Behind him in the distance the train whistle faded, the hurrying cars disappeared from sight. And Bongo at last was free!

On down the hillside he sped, and into the woods he had dreamed of for so long. Bongo was wide-eyed at the wonder of this new world. For the trees towered taller than circus tent poles. The flowers were brighter than colored balloons. The crisp air smelled better than popcorn and fresh-roasted peanuts. It was wonderful!

"Yes, sir, this is the life for me!" said Bongo.

He felt so good that he just had to run and jump and sniff and snort. He even tried to climb a tree, but, plunk! down he came, flat on his back.

Poor Bongo—he had never even seen a
tree before, except through the windows of
the circus train.

"Well," said Bongo, "I guess that takes a
little practice!"

He backed away again, and took another
little run. And plunk! Down he fell!

Now the branches above him were filled with twitterings and chatterings. The little woodland animals had all come out to meet Bongo.

"Hello," said Bongo shyly. "Let's be friends."

They taught him which were the most fragrant flowers to sniff. They showed him how to peek at his reflection in a quiet pool.

"I've never had so much fun," Bongo told them happily. "Your forest is wonderful."

And as the sun dropped behind the trees, Bongo looked up at the velvet sky twinkling with stars, while all around him stretched the sleepy quiet of the woods.

"Yes, this is the life for me," Bongo yawned contentedly, as he curled up for a good sleep.

He dozed off, but soon he woke up with a start. The night, which had seemed so peaceful, was full of sounds. Far off somewhere a coyote howled. Just then a chilly gust of wind shivered through the forest.

"Maybe this wood is not the place for me after all," he thought lonesomely.

Then storm clouds blotted out the stars. Across the inky blackness, yellow lightning flashed, and thunder rumbled angrily. Cold, soaking rain poured down on poor Bongo.

"I wish I'd never left the circus," he thought. At last, though, the rain did stop. The clouds parted, and a friendly moon shone through. And Bongo slept.

He woke up next morning, stiff as a board and cranky as an old bear—and hungry! He tried picking berries, but they were not very filling. Then he tried fishing, but the fish all got away.

At last he turned from the pool with a discouraged sigh. But what was this?

Right before his very eyes Bongo saw another little bear. And the bear was smiling at him!

For a moment Bongo thought he must be dreaming. He pinched himself, but the little bear was still there. So Bongo scampered over to get acquainted.

"Hello," he said shyly. "My name is Bongo." And he tipped his little circus cap.

"My name is Lulubelle," said the other little bear. "Let's play something."

This was wonderful. For the first time in his life Bongo had a playmate! Off they went through the woods together.

Bongo was so busy thinking how happy he

was that he didn't pay much attention to the crashing of underbrush and the crunching of stones as Lumpjaw, the biggest, toughest bear in the forest, came stamping out.

"H-hello," said Bongo shyly. Perhaps this was another playmate, he thought.

Lumpjaw did not bother to speak. He just swung one great paw at the little bear, and bong! Bongo crashed against a tree trunk, headfirst! As he pulled himself to his feet and shook his dizzy head, Lumpjaw lunged forward to hit him again.

But Bongo's new friend stepped between them. While Lumpjaw fumed, she stepped up to Bongo—and slapped him soundly on the cheek.

Bongo couldn't believe it. But it was true enough. So that there could be no mistake, the bear he thought his friend slapped him on the other cheek.

Bongo's heart was broken. He turned and slowly rode away. He did not dream that when he did this, it hurt the feelings of his friend. For no one had ever told him the ways of bears. How could he know that when a bear likes another bear, he says it with a slap?

Off into the woods went Bongo, heartsick.

"I should never have left the circus," said Bongo to himself. "Nobody likes me here." And he sighed.

Soon, as Bongo rode along, he heard near by the pounding rhythm of heavy feet. It sounded as though they were dancing. And he heard deep voices rumbling in what sounded like a song.

Quietly Bongo crept to the edge of an open clearing. The clearing was full of bears, a double line of them. They were shuffling about in a clumsy bear dance, and singing a tuneless bear song, and exchanging clumsy bear slaps.

"Why, they're slapping each other," Bon- go whispered to himself in surprise. "And they're not cross. They like each other!"

Then the words of the song reached him—

"Every pigeon likes to coo
When he says, 'I like you,'
But a bear likes to say it with a slap."

"With a slap!" cried Bongo. "Then Lulu-belle—she likes me! We're still friends!"

So Bongo raced out into the clearing, where his playmate was dancing with Lumpjaw, and gave her a sound slap.

Bongo's friend was delighted, but not Lumpjaw. He did not want any strange bear making friends with his playmate. He roared. He snorted. He fumed. He chased Bongo through the forest, tearing up trees and hurling them at the little bear as he went.

Up the mountainside raced Bongo, with Lumpjaw close behind him. Down the other side Bongo hustled, while the great rocks Lumpjaw was hurling rolled past him.

Lumpjaw cornered Bongo at last, on the edge of a cliff. There they teetered and tottered and struggled and fought, until Cr-r-runch! Sw-w-wish! Spl-lash!

The rock beneath them crumbled away, and they tumbled down, down, down, into a roaring river.

Now the other bears gathered on the river bank far above to watch as Lumpjaw and Bongo rode the current on a twirling, plunging log.

Closer and closer they came to the great white-foaming falls. The watching bears all held their breath! Then over the falls tumbled the great log, with Lumpjaw still clinging to it! Over the falls and down the river went the log and the bear, until at last they floated out of sight!

And Bongo? All the bears shook their heads and sighed when they thought of him.

But wait! What was this? Up the steep river bank a wet little bear came climbing, with a dripping little circus cap still upon his head. Yes, it was Bongo, a tired Bongo, but a proud and happy little bear.

"I'm back," he told Lulubelle, and he said it with a real bear slap.

"I'm glad," said his friend, with a pat that knocked him down.

"This is the life," cried Bongo happily, as he scrambled back to his feet again. "This is more fun than the circus ever was. Yes, sir, this is the life for me!"

He felt so good that he juggled a handful of pine cones, and he did a little dance with a twisty twig for a cane.

Then his new friends showed him where to find the fattest, sweetest grubs to eat, and a honey tree running over with delicious honey. And they found him a cave that was dry and warm, and just right for him.

"This is the life," cried Bongo happily. And he threw his little old circus cap away, high up into the branches of a tree.

"Yes, sir," said he, "I'm Bongo the woods bear now!"

BABES IN TOYLAND

THE GOOD FOLK of Mother Goose Village were excited and delighted. Beautiful Mary Contrary and handsome Tom the Piper were soon to be wed. In the village square, Mother Goose was giving a grand feast for them, and everyone was there.

In all the excitement, no one noticed that Barnaby and his two henchmen were watching from the attic of Barnaby's house.

Wicked Barnaby! He had a secret. Mary did not know it, but soon she would be an heiress. Soon she would be very wealthy. "I must have Mary's money," thought Barnaby.

Then he turned to his henchmen. One was called Gonzorgo, and he was very fat. The other was called Roderigo. He wasn't fat at all. But both were very wicked . . . why, they were almost as wicked as Barnaby.

"If you steal Miss Mary's sheep and then dispose of Tom," the wicked miser told them, "I'll pay you very well. Mary, you see, will think that she is poor. Without Tom, she'll have to marry me!"

As soon as the celebration in the square was over, the two greedy scoundrels set out to do Barnaby's bidding.

They followed when Tom walked Mary home.

They waited while Tom and Mary said good night.

But when Tom started back through Mary's garden gate, they seized him. Quick as a wink they had Tom trussed up in a sack. Then they put him into a wheelbarrow.

"We're on our way to take Tom and throw him in the sea," they sang. "And when the job is finally done, we'll get a handsome fee."

BUMP, BUMP, BUMP went poor Tom in the wheelbarrow as Gonzorgo and Roderigo pushed him along. At last they came to a crossroads. TO THE SEA and TO GYPSY CAMP, said the signposts.

Gonzorgo had a brilliant idea! "Why not sell Tom to the gypsies?" he said. "Then Barnaby will pay us for taking Tom away, and the gypsies will pay us for giving Tom to them. We'll be paid twice for the same job!"

Roderigo agreed. And off they went to the gypsy camp.

Early the next morning, Gonzorgo and Roderigo hurried to Mary's house. Barnaby was already there. The wicked wretch said he had come to wish Tom and Mary happiness.

Pretending to be sailors, Gonzorgo and Roderigo told Mary a sad tale. "Tom was at sea with us last night when a sudden storm came up. Alas," lamented Gonzorgo, "it washed him overboard."

Mary was stunned. "But why did Tom run off to sea?"

"He was poor," explained Gonzorgo. "Unable to support you, he ran away to set you free. Now you can marry wealthy Barnaby."

"That's an excellent suggestion," said the sly Barnaby.

Kindly, but firmly, Mary refused Barnaby. She did not want wealth. The sheep had always given her family a livelihood.

At that moment Bo Peep appeared, tears streaming down her pretty face. "I have lost the sheep!" she cried. "What will we do?"

Gonzorgo and Roderigo had successfully carried out the other part of Barnaby's evil scheme!

"Never mind, Bo Peep," soothed Mary. "You'll find them again."

"But they went into the Forest of No Return!" Bo Peep sobbed.

"How horrible!" cried Mary.

Barnaby smirked. "How will you and your brothers and sisters get along now? Perhaps

you should consider my offer again." And he took himself off to his crooked house, leaving Mary in great distress.

Indeed, how would Mary get on now? Without the sheep, she had no income at all! She tucked her little brothers and sisters into bed that night, assuring them that all would be well. But Mary herself was not so sure, and the children knew it.

Later, from their bedroom window, they watched Mary walk into the garden. She stopped and looked at Barnaby's crooked house, where a single dim light burned in the attic window. Then, very slowly, Mary began to walk toward that evil, beckoning light.

"She's going to marry Barnaby!" said one of the children.

"We must stop her!" said another.

"If we could find the sheep, she wouldn't have to marry him," suggested a third, feeling very brave. "Come on. Let's go!"

CLING! CLANG! CLING! Wildly, Gonzorgo and Roderigo rang the town bell. "Wake up, everybody! Wake up!" they shouted. CLING! CLANG! CLING! "Good news! Good news!"

The sleepy townspeople tumbled out of bed and ran to the square. There was Barnaby, smiling his crooked smile. And there was poor Mary, sad and pale, her hand caught fast in Barnaby's damp grip.

The good people of Mother Goose Village were shocked and silent when Barnaby announced his news. He and Mary were to be married!

"Don't grieve for Tom," she said, peering at Mary's palm. "He's alive!" Suddenly the gypsy threw off her tatters. It was Tom in disguise! Mary rushed into his arms and cried with happiness.

Barnaby was furious! Quickly, he ran off in search of the double-crossers. No more mistakes would be made. He would see to that!

Suddenly a band of gypsies burst into the square and began to sing and dance. Barnaby had hired them to help celebrate his betrothal.

Gonzorgo and Roderigo stared at them in horror. These were the same gypsies who had bought Tom! Terrified, they hid. Would Barnaby discover their deception?

The dancing was at its wildest when an old gypsy fortune teller came forth and beckoned to Mary.

Together, the happy couple walked to Mary's house. But bad news awaited them. Pinned to the door was a note from the children.

"Dear Sweet Mary," it said, "please don't marry Barnaby. We have gone to the Forest of No Return to find our lost sheep."

Horrified, Tom and Mary set out after the children. In their haste, they didn't notice the three silent shadows that followed them into the gloomy, forbidding forest.

Through the lonely, sighing woods, Tom and Mary searched. The night was at its blackest when at last they found the children, huddled together in a clearing.

The children were overjoyed to see their rescuers, and to know that Tom was still alive. "We're so happy to see you!" they cried. "We've been so afraid. The trees in this awful forest move and speak! They told us we could never leave here!"

"Now, now," Mary soothed. "It was only your imagination."

"Let's stay here until daybreak," suggested Tom. "When it is light enough, we'll find the sheep and then go home. You'll see."

Mary gathered the children to her and crooned a lullaby. Before long, the children's heads were nodding. Even Tom was asleep.

Only Barnaby and his henchmen, hidden behind some bushes, watched through the night.

The next morning, Tom and Mary awoke to find themselves surrounded by trees. They really did move. And they really did speak.

"This is the Forest of No Return," a tall pine told Tom. "Those who stumble in, those who fumble in, never can get out! The Toymaker in Toyland must decide your fate."

Suddenly the children forgot their fear. The very thought of seeing Toyland delighted them. "We're really going to go there?" they asked the trees. "You won't change your minds, will you?"

"Of course not! Line up right now!" directed an oak.

The trees marched Tom and Mary and the children off to Toyland. Along the way they all sang, loud and clear.

"Toyland! Toyland! Dear little
girl and boy land.
While you dwell within it, you are
ever happy then.
Childhood's Toyland, wonderful
world of joy land.
Once you leave its borders, you can
never return again."

Suddenly, there before them was Toyland! The children had never seen anything so wonderful! Fantastic toy figures and a hundred weather vanes covered the big white house that stood in the center of an island.

Tom led the children across the bridge, past the toy sentries that guarded the open gates, and up to the door of the Toy Factory.

There they saw a sign: CLOSED FOR ALTERATIONS. Although no one answered his knock, Tom heard voices coming from inside.

The voices belonged to the Toymaker and Grumio, his assistant. Grumio had just invented a toy-making machine, and he was showing the Toymaker how it worked.

"You push a button for the things you want. For a girl doll, push Sugar, Spice, Everything Nice, and Golden Hair," Grumio explained. He demonstrated by punching the buttons himself.

The machine began snorting and chuffing. Motors turned, pistons and arms whirled, and lights flashed. Sweet music filled the air —and a little Dutch doll dropped out.

"But," Grumio cautioned the Toymaker, "it's a very delicate machine. You must be careful not to overload it."

The Toymaker, eager to test the invention, didn't hear Grumio's advice. He pushed buttons for Boat . . . Block . . . Train . . . Airplane . . . Toy Soldier. . . .

Whistles screeched, rockets went off, and a neon sign flashed. The Toymaker had overloaded the machine! The arms and pistons flew off in a great explosion.

When the smoke had cleared away, all that was left of the machine was dust.

"Oh, dear!" said the Toymaker, picking himself up and brushing the dust from his coat. "It's half past October, and no toys are ready yet. It may be a very sad Christmas."

At that moment, Tom stepped forward and introduced himself. He said that if the children could help with the toys, the Toymaker might have the presents ready in time after all.

The Toymaker agreed, and soon the children were working on an assembly line. They painted smiles on the dolls' faces and wrapped the other toys in big gay packages.

In the evening, Tom and Mary tucked the little workers into makeshift beds in the storeroom. As they all went to sleep, evil Barnaby lurked nearby, waiting to kidnap Mary.

After everyone was deep in slumber, Grumio burst in on the Toymaker! He had invented a special formula that would reduce an object to the size of a toy

Overjoyed, the Toymaker filled a spray gun with the formula and aimed it at his bed. POOF! A toy-sized bed! POOF! A chair turned into a miniature chair! POOF! POOF! POOF! The Toymaker poofed everything in sight.

Standing in the room full of toys, the Toymaker said, "Grumio, you're a genius!"

Then the Toymaker became unhappy. "Where am I going to get enough big things to make into small things?" he wondered. Then he turned to Grumio. "This thing is no help to me at all, Grumio. You and your silly inventions!"

Discouraged and unhappy, the Toymaker threw Grumio's poof-gun out the bedroom window.

Standing just outside was Barnaby, who picked up the gun with a nasty chuckle. It would help him to carry out his evil scheme.

The first thing Barnaby did was point the gun at the Toymaker. POOF! The Toymaker was toy-size!

Gonzorgo and Roderigo were shocked. Realizing that Barnaby intended to use the gun on everyone, they had a change of heart. "We want nothing more to do with this horrible plot," they told him.

"Then I will turn the poof-gun on you!" replied Barnaby.

Barnaby pointed the gun at his former friends.

Gonzorgo and Roderigo hid behind a huge barrel. POOF! The barrel was toy-size, and they loomed like giants behind it.

Then Barnaby took aim once more. POOF! The formula hit Roderigo! POOF! The formula hit Gonzorgo! Barnaby picked up the two fleeing men between his thumb and forefinger and deposited them in a bird cage.

Next on Barnaby's list was Tom. POOF! In the wink of an eye, Tom became only six inches high!

Then Barnaby found his way to Mary. He hovered over her like a big black bird. Frightened, Mary screamed for Tom.

Laughing an evil laugh, Barnaby plucked Tom out of his pocket and set him down near the bird cage. Poor Tom! He was all tied up with red ribbon. Barnaby turned to Mary with a sneer. "Now I will have your hand in marriage!" he commanded.

"Never!" sobbed Mary. "Never!"

"Oh, yes!" countered Barnaby. "May I remind you that one more shot of this formula will make Tom disappear—forever!"

Mary had no choice. "The marriage will take place immediately!" said Barnaby. "The Toymaker will marry us."

When the ceremony started, Tom inched closer to the cage. It was a simple matter for Gonzorgo to untie Tom's bonds.

Free once more, Tom jumped to a chair and then to the floor. He slipped through a crack in the door and ran into the shipping room. First he cut the ribbons on all the boxes. Then he blew a call to arms on a toy trumpet.

Row on row of toy soldiers fell into line. Battleships and cannons, Trojans and Indians —all answered the call.

Tom and his toy army arrived in the workshop just as Barnaby and Mary were about to be pronounced man and wife.

"Stop!" shouted Tom. Telling Mary to take cover, he jumped on his hobby horse and led the troops into battle.

The battleship fired, filling Barnaby's mouth with marbles.

The Indians unloosed their arrows, and the suction cups stuck to Barnaby's nose.

But Barnaby fought back. With his foot, he swept the whole army off its wooden feet. He hurled a battleship into a pail of water, and its toy admiral sank to the bottom. Reaching for the toy soldiers, he hurled them against the wall.

"Enough of this horse play," Barnaby muttered, and he pulled out the poof-gun. He planned to reduce everything to oblivion.

Then a zeppelin flew over, and dropped its load of marbles.

The marbles proved to be Barnaby's undoing. While the wicked fellow was slipping and sliding on them, Mary picked up a discarded toy gunboat and put a marble in its cannon.

POW! The marble met its mark. It shattered the poof-gun, and the liquid spattered all over Barnaby.

Now that Barnaby was toy-size, Tom attacked once more. Tom, with his sword, and Barnaby, with his crooked cane, fought back and forth over the littered floor of the Toy Factory. They parried and thrust for many long minutes, but Tom's skill with the sword finally overcame Barnaby's sly tricks.

Tom maneuvered Barnaby toward an open box. One quick lunge and—BOOM!—Barnaby fell backward, right into the box. Tom leaped forward and shut the lid. At last, Barnaby was a prisoner!

The soldiers all cheered Tom's victory. The toys would never forget what he had done.

No sooner was the battle over than Grumio ran into the room. He had another new invention—a magic restoring formula.

"This is just what we need!" said the Toymaker. "I'm sorry I scolded you before, Grumio," he went on. "Please forgive me."

Grumio sprayed the new formula all around the room, restoring the toy furniture to its full size.

He sprayed it on the Toymaker and Tom, who returned to their regular height.

Then he unlocked the bird cage and freed Gonzorgo and Roderigo. He sprayed them, too.

Grumio sprayed all the wounded and broken soldiers, and they became as good as new. Their red coats were as bright as ever, and their guns were straight again. The toy admiral was hale and hearty—and dry!

He sprayed it on everybody—except Barnaby, who was still safely inside the box.

In fact, Grumio's new formula made it possible for all the toys to be ready in time for Christmas. And the Toymaker was so happy that he pinned a great big Hero Medal on Grumio's chest.

A few days later, back in Mother Goose Village, there was another celebration. It was in honor of Tom and Mary's wedding.

Mother Goose held the Toymaker's bird cage in her hand, and inside the cage was Barnaby. He was still toy-size—and that's the way they intended to keep him.

And so Tom and Mary were married, and lived happily ever after . . . with the Babes in Toyland.

Mary's House

Mother Goose Village

Forest of No Return

Barnaby's House

Toyland